THE ARCANE ULTIMATUM

ANDREW S. FRENCH

NEONOIR BOOKS

ALSO BY ANDREW S. FRENCH

The Arcane Supernatural Thriller Series

Book one: The Arcane

Book two: The Arcane Identity

Book three: The Arcane Quest

Book four: The Arcane Ultimatum

The Ella Finn Fantasy Novella Series

Ella and the Elementals

Ella and the Multiverse

Ella and the Monsters

Ella and the Dreamers

Supernatural Short Stories

Dead Souls

The Shadow

Science Fiction

The Time Traveller's Murder

The Mercy Sleep

Bodies

The Astrid Snow series

Book one: Don't Fear the Reaper

Book two: The Killing Moon

Book three: Lost in America

Book four: Gone to Texas

Book five: The Final Girl

The Detective Jen Flowers series

Book one: The Hashtag Killer

Book two: Serial Killer

Book three: Night Killer

Book four: The Killer Inside Them

Northern Crime Fiction

Where The Bodies Are Buried

The Ophelia Red series

Book one: Ophelia Red

Crime Short Stories

Call Me: An Astrid Snow Short Story

Dark Snow: An Astrid Snow Short Story

Bette Davis Eyes: Detective Flowers Short Story

Go to www.andrewsfrench.com for more information.

1 ALICE: MYSTERY TRAIN

An hour after my escape from the Devil, my mother drank her small bottle of wine in one go. She smacked her lips and grinned at me. 'You don't know how much you enjoy something until it's taken from you.'

I munched on my cheese sandwich and wondered if she was talking about her children, of me and my identical twin, Cassie. Sixteen years ago, perhaps only a few hours after our birth, we'd been smuggled out of the hospital and away from two warring archangels who wanted us for their own devious plans: the Archangel Michael and his sister, the Devil herself, Lucy, also known as the First of the Fallen and the Morningstar. Doubtless, she had other names and forms, but to me, she was the Queen of Lies, the one who'd stolen my mother from me; the one who'd left my sister to her fate in America.

There was a ringing in my ears, like a radio station playing music you hate; a reminder of what we'd escaped from inside Buckingham Palace, of leaving Lucy behind before she could kill my mother. But it wasn't just the noise of the explosions and the screams of those Lucy had killed; it was the sound of my guilt for who I'd abandoned: Bella.

Bella, Dracula's sister, the vampire who'd got me to my mother and who I'd left fighting with her brother inside the royal palace.

But what else could I have done?

The countryside whizzed by outside as I kept my face close to the window. The First Class carriage was empty apart from us and an old couple at the back, which I was happy about. I was still a wanted fugitive in the British Isles, so I couldn't let our current good fortune distract me from that.

I peered at my mother as she licked the wine across her lips, reminiscent of the blood I'd had to drink just to be able to teleport us away from Lucy. It was the Devil's blood, the taste of which still lingered at the back of my throat and tickled at a shadowy voice hiding in the dark corners of my mind.

'We need to get to America and find Cassie.'

I didn't understand how to speak to her as my mother. We'd hugged and held hands, but I struggled for words and emotion, and I sensed it was the same for her. Even after sixteen years apart, this wasn't the best time for a family reunion. It was easier to concentrate on the tasks at hand, and they were considerable.

She smiled at me. 'We will, Alice, as soon as we have the right resources.'

I reached for my orange juice, conscious of my damp shirt after scrubbing Lucy's dried blood off me.

'Why are we heading to Leeds?' I had a million and one questions for her, but settled on the easiest.

'We're going to the Foundation. They'll have everything we need to stay safe from Lucy and her minions and find your sister.' The lack of warmth in her words disturbed me, but I put it down to the anxiety she must have been feeling since I felt it too.

I tried my best to make light of the situation. 'Are they a charity for abandoned supernatural creatures?'

A soft curve of her lips revealed the top row of her teeth. 'It's something like that; only the Foundation tries to help all of life's unfortunates, regardless of whom or what they are.'

'How do you know this place since you spent sixteen years imprisoned in Hell?'

Pride sparkled in her face. 'The Foundation is my creation.' She pushed the empty wine bottle to the side. 'Numerous creatures of the supernatural are immortal, yet do nothing with their longevity. I wanted to use it to improve the lives of as many as possible. When you've lived for so long, if you can avoid the pitfalls of those trying to enslave or murder you, it's easy to acquire wealth and influence. Then, what you do with those things is what's important. But, everything has been so much harder than it should have because I've had to stay hidden in the background.'

'Hidden from whom?' I'd heard this story from others, but I wanted to hear it from her.

'God may have abandoned this world and all life on it, but the Creator's acolytes are many, and once it became known the last of the Nephilim had survived the Great Flood, there was nothing they wouldn't do to track me down and end me.'

'God's acolytes? You mean the churches?'

'I mean every religion on the planet, every one of the devout and devoted, seeking me with feverish zeal. Eventually, I had to quit running to defend myself and help others in my situation.'

'What do you mean by others? I thought you were the last of the Nephilim?'

'I am, but once the fundamentalists take the first step to persecution, they don't stop with one minority; they feast their fears and frustrations on all the others. So I created the Foundation to fight back for me and millions like me. I was doing this when something wonderful happened.'

'What was that?'

Her smile grew broader and brighter than the sun. 'I discovered I was pregnant.'

The train slowed to a stop as we came to a station. I stared at her and didn't know what to say. Some teenagers stumbled into the carriage before falling back out, laughing when they realised it was First Class.

'You were pregnant with Cassie and me?'

She opened her second bottle of wine and laughed. 'Well, I was unaware it was twins at the time, but, yes, it was you and your sister and nobody else.'

The red liquid pouring into the plastic glass reminded me of Lucy's blood.

Then the voice slithered out of the corner of my mind and whispered to me.

You should have kept the blood. Then you could have teleported the two of you to Leeds instead of wasting time on this train.

'I've never been to Leeds.'

My reply was to the imaginary voice in my head, but my mother must have thought it was for her.

'It's a beautiful city, full of life and vibrancy, and you get a much warmer welcome than down south.'

'What happened with the pregnancy? How did you end

up in that hospital? Who smuggled Cassie and me from there, away from the clutches of Michael and Lucy?'

She sipped at her drink. 'I'd kept my whereabouts secrets for centuries until someone betrayed me to the archangels.' Her hands shook as she spoke. 'The pregnancy was tough. I shouldn't have been surprised by that. I carried the Arcane within me, but circumstances overtook the preparations for the birth.'

'What circumstances? Who betrayed you?'

My mother ran her fingers around the plastic glass, her eyes avoiding mine for a second before peering deep into me.

'There were complications with the pregnancy. We didn't have enough facilities at the Foundation then, so my doctor urged your father to take me to the nearest hospital. The last thing I remember was him driving me there before I blacked out.' She finished the drink, a look of contemplation possessing her face. 'I only found out the rest later. Lucy took great pleasure in torturing me with the truth.'

The train shuddered over the tracks as irritation crept through my veins. 'And why would you believe her? She told me many lies about you.'

'I'm sure she did, but I heard the truth from your father's lips.'

The carriage juddered again and I banged my leg into the side of the seat. 'My father told you?'

'Not directly. Lucy showed me the interrogation clips where Michael did his best to get your father to reveal you and your sister's location.'

'Videos are easy to fake.'

'That's true, but I recognised the pain in your father's face when he spoke.' Her voice was loud enough for the old couple to look in our direction. 'He spirited my children away from the hospital and betrayed my whereabouts to those warring archangels.'

'Why would he do that?' I found myself defending a man I'd never met.

'Your father is – was - an archangel himself and the entire angel community is split regarding God's return to this world. You and Cassie were to be his offerings to the Creator, a gift to cement his place at the feet of the great murderer.' She turned her face to the window, her reflection bubbling with enough anger, I thought the glass would buckle and melt.

I leant back into my seat and didn't know what to think. None of this made any difference in finding my sister and rescuing her from an American prison.

'How will we travel to America and locate Cassie?'

My mother seemed glad about the change of subject. 'First, you need to tell me everything about you before we get to Leeds.' She tapped the side of her head. 'Knowledge is power.'

If you'd kept some of Lucy's blood, you could have used it to read her mind and discover the truth of what she's saying.

I finished the rest of the juice, hoping once Lucy's blood was out of my body, this annoying voice in my brain would disappear. I settled into my seat and told my mother my life story, from my first memory until getting into Buckingham Palace. By the time we arrived at Leeds, she was gazing at me in appreciation.

'I have nothing but admiration for you, Alice, for surviving all that.' She stepped off the train and I followed her. She pulled me to one side as the other passengers slipped by. 'But you'll never have to be alone again, my daughter.' She placed her fingers on my face. 'And I promise we'll bring Cassie home safely once we have the resources for the job.' She held my hand as we exited the station.

The city centre was to our right, but she took us left and across the road.

'How do you know this Foundation will be there after all this time?'

We stopped at the traffic lights and she let go of me. She reached into her trouser pocket and removed a phone. 'I've been in touch with them since Dracula gave me the puppy eyes and did everything I asked him to.'

'They still have the same number?'

'I don't know. I searched for them on the internet. They've grown since I was there.' She was about to cross the road until I stopped her.

'What happened between you and Dracula?'

A police car screeched past us and I hid my face from it. When it had gone, my mother appeared pensive.

'Understand, Alice, I was trapped in Hell for sixteen years, which seemed like sixteen eternities. Dracula needed companionship and I wanted freedom, so I was happy enough to swap Lucy's imprisonment for the vampire's controlling presence.'

'But you changed roles with him?'

'It didn't take long. Dracula is a deeply lonely creature, full of sadness and sorrow. I think it was an eternity since he'd experienced true love. There were plenty of fawning acolytes ready to do anything for him, both human and vampire. Still, once I'd adjusted to my new situation, it was easy for me to use my charm on such a pitiful individual.'

Even though I hardly knew this woman, the thought of her, of my mother, in a romantic entanglement with Dracula made my stomach churn.

'Whose idea was it to relocate to Buckingham Palace?'

We continued to stand on the pavement as the world passed us by.

She looked at me with what appeared to be respect. 'The poor boy is so scared of you and Cassie, he's prepared to do anything and go anywhere to escape you. I thought I'd use the opportunity to meet some influential people who would help me find you and your sister.'

'Lucy told me you were there to use the Royal Family to reveal the truth about the supernatural.'

Mother grabbed her face and let out a laugh loud enough to worry those standing opposite, a Christian couple handing out leaflets about Jesus and the Second Coming.

'Now, why on earth would I do something as silly as that?'

'You want revenge against God for trying to kill you, and this was your way of gathering an army for that purpose.'

'Does that make any sense to you?'

I shook my head. 'No, it doesn't. I've learnt the hard way not to trust the Queen of Lies.'

We crossed the road together. A group of women celebrating a Hen Party staggered towards us. I dodged the giant inflatable plastic male genitals and hurried after my mother.

'All I want is the best for you and Cassie, Alice. We've got a lot of missing time to make up for.' She turned left and away from the people heading for the pubs and restaurants. There was a large building ahead of us with the word University stamped into the concrete. We kept on walking past it and towards an area looking like an industrial estate.

'Where is this Foundation of yours?'

She pointed up the road. 'There.'

'That's a TV studio.'

'Beyond that, it's the place with all the grass on the walls.'

I gazed at the bizarre structure. 'Really?'

My mother put her arm around my shoulder and squeezed my hand.

'Our future is green, Alice.'

2 CASSIE: ANGELS

I stood inside a prison cell with a broken angel. It was a hell of a way to meet my father.

He moved his withered bony frame from the wall, the stink of rotten eggs drifting from his rags. His thick grey beard appeared to be alive until I realised insects were moving through it. I dragged my gaze from them and to the scars underneath his eyes, pale blue ones staring at me. He held one hand out to me, but I didn't take it.

'My father is dead.' The words stumbled out of my mouth as if they were crawling over broken glass.

There was a glint in his pupils as he replied. 'Rumours of my demise are many and unfounded. I am Gabriel, your father.'

I turned from his gaze to stare at the walls. 'Where am I?'

The chain rattled as he spoke, his voice wavering. 'This is no place for you, my daughter; you should use your powers to leave now.'

I placed my hand on the wall, the cold adding to the chill in my heart.

'I have no powers. I'm stuck here with you.' I ran my fingers across the stone, flakes falling away and drifting to the floor; the cell stank of decay and desperation. I squashed the vomit crawling from my gut. His face shrank, his eyes like hollow husks.

'Then there is no hope for either of us.'

'How did you get here?' If he got in, there must be a way out.

His fragile frame shook as he spoke. 'The angels build the cells around you.' Another howl of despair erupted outside. 'We are fleshless and eternal, but inside a human body, we can do anything they can, and more.'

'Is this your human form?' I tried not to think of him as my father.

'This is my final form. My Grace was torn from me, same as my wings.' He pulled from the wall and turned his back to me. Severed bones protruded from his shoulders with small bloodstained feathers sticking to them.

The sickness grew in me. 'And what happened to the person inside it?'

A sea of sorrow swam across the scars on his face. 'An angel never inhabits a body without permission. It is a great honour for a human to be chosen by an angel as its vessel.'

'What happens to the person when the angel takes over?'

'They ascend to a higher plane. This human's soul is in Heaven, or at least it was.'

'What does that mean?'

'The gates of Heaven are closed. I don't know what happened to the souls there, but no more are allowed inside until the war is over.'

'A war between who?'

'It's a war between those who await God's return and

welcome the Creator's plan to wash the Earth clean, and those who oppose such a terrible thing.'

This was what Lucy and Michael had told me; why both of them wanted to control Alice and me. But when I'd mentioned this to the Demon Lord Aziz, he'd said it was a fairy tale spread by the angels to intimidate others. Even after everything I'd seen and encountered, I was still struggling to believe such a God existed.

'I thought all angels were servants of God.'

Gabriel shook his head. 'No. From the earliest days of Creation, there has been rebellion.'

'Are you talking about Satan?'

'And others.'

The conversation made me think about Lucy again and how she'd betrayed Alice and me. My body ached with the thought of what might have happened to my sister. But at least she wasn't stuck in this cell with me.

'You said the gates of Heaven are closed to all, so what happens to people when they die? Where do their souls go?'

'There are more things than Heaven and Hell.'

'Are you talking about Limbo and Purgatory? I've been to both of them.'

'That's only two of numerous realms. God designed countless places for Their creations to exist, building a hierarchy of levels, different planes of existence. I can only assume the human dead are going to one or more of those while the war rages.'

Maybe that's what Wovoka meant when he mentioned there being many spirit worlds. The thought of him tugged at my heart, of the sacrifice he and Sayan had made to take Michael through those realms of the departed.

I glanced around the cell again. 'So where is this place, this Devastation?'

His eyes were black when I'd arrived, but now they glistened with light blue. It reminded me of Pandora's azure mist and I shivered.

'This prison sits on the edge of the Celestial Garden, a Garden long since burnt to the ground.'

I considered what he'd said while I contemplated the most pressing matter: how to get away and find Alice. I closed my eyes and concentrated on being in Whitby. My forehead contracted and I squeezed my skull as much as possible, resisting the temptation to click my heels three times. I pushed until my brain throbbed, but nothing happened. The Arcane abilities I'd used to defeat Pandora had vanished again. If they only appeared during moments of stress, they should reappear soon enough.

'How old are you?' Gabriel said.

My eyes flicked open, my nails digging into my palms. 'I'm sixteen.'

His gaze sprang wide, icy breath spurting from his mouth. 'You're too young to have travelled through space to here. How did you do it?'

I told him about Sayan and the flower. 'I'm not sure why it brought me here.'

'Blood will find blood, Cassie, and I am yours.'

'You keep saying that, but where's the proof?'

He placed one finger into the palm of his other hand and drew his nail across it, cutting into his skin until red trickled out and dripped over the ground.

'The shaman was correct. My blood brought you here because it flows through both of us. Why you came to me and not your sister or mother is perplexing and unfortunate, but here you are.' He held his hand up to me. 'What more proof do you need than that?'

I wasn't prepared to admit to anything. 'I'll be the judge of that.'

His eyes were like pinpricks in the half-light. 'Have you experienced any of your Arcane abilities yet?'

Should I tell him what had happened to me since meeting my twin sister? Cold drifted off the walls and I guessed I wouldn't be going anywhere soon. So I recounted Lucy's training, about the fight in the bunker, my stint in the American prison, and Pandora. He listened intently, never asking questions, though it appeared he wanted to. At the back of my throat, I still tasted Pandora.

'It was the blood that awakened your Arcane gifts.'

I didn't like the sound of that. 'What do you mean?'

'You're too young to do these things, Cassie; they'll come in time. But certain blood, which originated from angels, can act as a drug to ignite your abilities earlier than they should be.' He pulled an insect from his beard and, much to my disgust, ate it. 'Lucy fed you blood when she pretended to train you. With Pandora, some of her blood must have got into your system when the two of you fought.' His eyes widened. 'You can't keep doing that; it will poison you eventually.'

'I don't intend to.' Though I would if it meant I could get away and return to Alice.

'So you're stuck here with me.' Tears dribbled into his beard. 'Maybe I should have left you both with your mother.'

'It was you who took us from the hospital?'

'I had to. It was the only way to keep you safe.'

'Why didn't you take us with you?'

'You still would have been in danger. I had to get you as far away as possible.'

'But why separate us?' Anger rippled through my veins.

'What? You were supposed to stay together. That's what I told the nurse.'

'What nurse?'

'Natasha. She worked at the Foundation.'

More confusion stabbed at my brain. A mist of cold wafted into the impregnable room.

'What Foundation?'

He was about to speak when he dropped to the ground, his hands pulling at his throat as his face bulged and spit fell over his lips. He was choking in front of me. I lunged forward to help him, only to be flung back by an invisible surge of electric energy. Agony rippled through my body, a pain I recognised from before; from the hospital when Lucy had tossed me against the wall. Was she here? My eyes danced around the cell in panic as Gabriel twitched and jerked on the ground. Something was killing him.

'Leave him alone,' I screamed.

Dark smoke blew to him at the far end of the cell, swirling in the air until it settled into a gaseous human form. It had no eyes, but long wispy arms and legs. In the centre of it was a small pulsating light. I lunged towards it, anger and confusion spurting me forward, and it fled through the concrete. I turned to help Gabriel, pushing my arm under his and dragging him up. He let out a great cough and smiled.

'You scared it away.'

'What was it?'

'It was one of my jailers.'

The realisation sank into me. 'That was the true form of an angel?'

He nodded. 'That was a Seraphim, the highest of the angels. I didn't recognise who it was, but the leaders never visit the cells.'

'It looked like the true form of a demon.'

He wiped the spit from his chin and laughed. 'Don't say that to them. Angels are twitchy about being compared to Satan's creations.'

'Was the light at the centre its Grace?'

He nodded again. 'It was.' Then I watched the sadness consume him once more. 'Grace is everything to us, like souls for humans. They took it from me as punishment before hacking my wings off me.'

'Why have they punished you?'

He smiled and touched my cheek. 'Because I helped you escape from them.' Then the light faded from his face. 'But now you're here and, without knowing how, I've delivered you into their arms.'

'Don't worry; I'll get us both out of here.' I said it with more confidence than I felt. I was considering its difficulties as the living smoke seeped through the wall, joined by another two. They glistened in the air before taking human shape. Even with no eyes, they stared at me as they hovered above the ground. They were tempting me to reach out and grab for the shimmering pinprick of light which was their Grace when they vanished again.

'They were examining you, Cassie. If you have a way out of here, take it now.'

But I didn't, not unless I was prepared to kick start my teleportation powers by drinking the blood of the man claiming to be my father. And I wouldn't do that.

Before I could react, a loud hammering came from the other side of the prison. Puffs of dust and plaster splattered around the cell. I grabbed hold of Gabriel's arm and pulled him as far away from the destruction as his chain would allow.

'They're huffing and puffing and blowing the wall

down,' I said, trying to ignore the seriousness of the situation. It didn't take long for it to collapse in front of us. When the dust settled, there were no wispy angels; only a tall, stocky man built like a bodybuilder. He wore an Armani suit over his impressive frame, his shoulder-length hair as snow white as his eyes. When he spoke, my skin shivered as if struck by lightning.

'What blasphemy is this, Gabriel?'

My father, if that's who he was, stood as straight as he could and stuck out his chest. 'This is more of your trickery, Seraphiel. I don't know who the girl is or how she got here.'

In a blink of an eye, Seraphiel had one hand around my neck. He lifted me off the ground and squeezed as my legs kicked against him, my arms flailing in the air. Spit fell from my mouth as my tongue shrank to the back of my throat. I dropped both hands to my chest and clutched at my heart.

'Your vision must be going the same way as your mind, Gabriel, if you don't recognise your daughter.' A milky white mist swirled in Seraphiel's pupils. 'What a coup this is for the Seraphim to put one of the Arcane on trial. All the Hosts in Heaven will sing of this day for eternity.'

As my eyes closed, a whispering voice sang a lullaby inside my head.

3 ALICE: THE FOUNDATION

I stood outside the Foundation, my eyebrows arching for the sky, mouth gaping wide at the sight of the front wall covered in greenery, flowers and plants sticking out from the side to breathe life into the city. It was as if giant hands had scooped up the whole of nature, sculpted it into the shape of an office block, and dropped it into the concrete jungle.

My mother walked up to the entrance. 'It's changed a lot since I was here last.' She turned to me. 'Let's see if it's as magnificent as this inside.'

She stepped through the door with me in quick pursuit. There wasn't as much nature indoors, but there was enough of it to add vibrant colours to the clear glass and starkness of the walls. An enormous fountain stood in the centre with water dripping into a pool at the bottom.

A man strode towards us, excitement in his step and his face. His curls were midnight black and his eyes dark brown; his prominent cheekbones were crafted from a fashion magazine. A doctor's uniform fitted tightly to his large frame. His name badge identified him as Dr Julius Silk.

'My God, Mary, you haven't changed a bit.'

He paused before my mother and I was sure he wanted to throw his arms around her. She put him out of his misery and grabbed his hands.

'And you're as handsome as ever, Julius.' They stood for a minute like lovers reunited after years apart, and I felt my cheeks sizzle. Then they separated and he stared at me.

'And this must be Alice.' He held his hand out to me. I took it, but for only a second, his flesh cold to the touch.

'This is some building you have,' I said.

He glanced around the structure. 'We thought it was about time the city had at least one green lung breathing life into it.'

Mother moved to the fountain. 'I can't believe what you've done here, Julius.' She turned to look at him. 'Has the work you've completed been as impressive as the facade of the Foundation?'

Dr Silk buried his hands in the pockets of his coat, a nervous tic flicking at his eyes. 'Just wait until you see our achievements, Mary; you'll be proud of your legacy.'

She glanced at me, and then back at him. 'Do you have living facilities here? Alice needs a shower and clean clothes. And I guess she's as hungry as I am.'

Silk lifted his arm and waved a young woman over. She wore the same uniform embroidered with the Foundation logo of a building rising from the rubble and touching the sky. She looked about five years older than me.

'Amy, take Alice to the residential quarters and find her some clean clothes; something about your size will do.'

She smiled at me. I looked to Mother for guidance; she nodded and headed in the opposite direction with Dr Silk. Their departure was the signal for Amy to speak to me.

'Do you want jeans, skirt or a dress?'

I scanned the rest of the room, searching for anything which might be helpful or interesting. There were half a dozen members of staff dressed the same way as Amy, some of them carrying folders and looking important, while others peered into tablet computers or smartphones.

'Jeans and a dark top will do.' The place reminded me of a modernist hospital, but there was one thing missing: there was no smell or aroma of anything. It was the cleanest building I'd ever been in; even Amy smelt of nothing.

'What about underwear?'

'What?'

'Do you have a preference for underwear, Alice? Do you want comfortable or pretty?'

This girl was funny. 'Can't they be both?'

She grinned. 'Not in my experience.' She placed her hand on my elbow and leant into me. 'Once I get you set up in a room, I'll pop into the town and purchase whatever you desire.'

'Okay.'

She kept on grinning as she led me from the main reception and towards a lift. Amy removed an ID card from her pocket and pressed it against the side of the lift. The door opened, and we stepped inside. There were twelve floors on the panel and she hit number six.

'I'll take you to one of the better suites.'

The metal box moved silently up. 'Do you live and work here?'

She laughed. 'Oh no; I have a place out in student land. It's small, but cheap.'

'What do you do here, Amy?'

Her answer wasn't instant. Then it was as if she was reading from an official memo.

'The Foundation exists to bring about social progress and to improve the lives of those who have the least.'

'Those are noble objectives, but how do you achieve them?'

Her blue eyes sparkled with excitement. 'Well, I'm only a low-level data cruncher, but I know experiments are going on here to produce food that will grow in the worst of conditions, and there are plans to develop abandoned land and buildings to provide shelter for the homeless. And I'm sure there are plenty of other things I'm not privy to.'

We came to a halt on the sixth floor. 'So, you don't offer job opportunities for vampires and werewolves?'

The door opened as wide as her eyes. She bit her lip, and then let out a roar of laughter. 'You're funny, Alice. Did someone tell you I'm a big *Twilight* fan?'

'No.'

She led me out of the lift. 'There are plenty of horrible people in Leeds, just like most places, but how marvellous would it be if vampires and werewolves existed?'

'Yes, fantastic.'

We walked down an empty corridor, past several rooms, until she stopped at the end. Amy pushed a door open and invited me in. It was better than anywhere I'd stayed during my search for Dracula and my mother: a large double bed, half-full bookcase, decent-sized TV on the wall, and a private bathroom.

'I'll let you relax and be back in an hour with those clothes. Will you be okay?'

I nodded and gave her my best smile. 'I'll be fine, thanks.'

She closed the door behind her. I looked for a lock, but there wasn't one. I sighed and flopped on the bed. At least my top had dried. I waited for the imaginary voice in my head to return, but it didn't. I guessed it meant my Lucy blood-instigated powers had vanished. I squeezed an image of flying above the clouds into my brain and tried to levitate, but nothing happened.

I kicked off my shoes and turned the TV on. The news channels were numerous, but none had any mention of an incident at Buckingham Palace. All I could think about was Bella and how I'd abandoned her. She was another in a long line that I'd let down, starting with Akemi in the park when that kid werewolf attacked us. Then there were my neighbours Bob and Terry, who'd died horrible deaths because of me; Sarda and the other prisoners I'd left behind in the Nexus who were now locked up in some government facility; plus those tortured souls in Limbo at the mercy of a demon army. And then there was Cassie, lost in America while I played happy families with a mother I hardly knew.

I muted the sound on the TV and reached for my phone, but the battery was dead. I should have asked Amy for a charger. I grabbed a pillow and pressed it to my face. Like the building, it smelt of nothing; the sheets on the bed were the same. It was as if the whole place had had every aroma sucked out of it. The cleanliness made me itch. Or perhaps it was because I hadn't showered in a while. I lifted my armpit and sniffed it; there was no disguising the bouquet in my flesh.

The wooded floor was cold against my bare feet as I slipped off the covers. My jacket dangled over the bed. I grabbed it and hung it on the back of the chair near the bookshelf. Something caught my eye as I did so; inside the lapel, reaching halfway down from the top, was a ruby stain against the leather. I placed my fingers over it.

It was Lucy's dried blood.

A tingle ran through my skin, penetrating my flesh and

attaching itself to muscle and bone. I snatched back from the jacket with a jerk. Then, somewhere in the shadows of my mind, a tiny echoing voice whispered to me.

Drink it. Drink it all.

My heart thumped against my ribs, the inside of my skull vibrating on an irritating frequency. I stumbled into the bathroom and pulled off my clothes. I dropped everything on the floor, leaning into the shower to turn it on. I left it to run hot and gazed into the mirror, for once not cringing at my reflection.

Energy leaked out of me as the water bounced off the tiles. There were lines under my eyes that hadn't been there before, my cheeks sallow and sunken. I'd been living off adrenalin for so long, I'd forgotten what real sustenance was. I climbed into the shower, pulled the curtain across, pushed my head into the wall and allowed the heat to nip my neck.

I don't know how long I stayed like that, but my skin was as wrinkled as parchment by the time I got out. There was a bathrobe on the back of the door. I put it on and went into the main room. There was a pile of clean clothes on the bed, plus a phone charger and a note from Amy.

Hi, Alice. I didn't want to disturb you. I hope you like these. I saw the battery was dead on your mobile, so I left you this. Your mother and Dr Silk want to show you something at six o'clock. And there'll be food. I'll come back for you then. Amy.

The time on the TV said ten minutes to six. I connected my phone to the charger and plugged it into a socket. Amy had left me functional dark underwear, which fitted me perfectly. The jeans were the duplicate of the ones I'd been wearing. A long-sleeved white top finished the combo. I wouldn't win any fashion awards, but it would do.

I was contemplating putting on my jacket when there was a knock on the door.

'Come in.'

Amy entered, the smile glued to her face. 'Are you ready to see your mother?'

'Sure,' I replied. 'And thanks for the clothes.' Like everything else, they smelt of nothing. But in my mind, I could still smell Lucy's blood on me.

'Come on, then; there's food waiting for you downstairs.'

We went back to the lift, her all smiles and me riddled with nerves, anticipation, and restlessness; the image of Cassie a permanent fixture at the forefront of my thoughts. I watched the numbers count down from six, expecting a bump when we hit zero, but we continued descending.

I turned to her. 'Are we going underground?'

Impish glee spread across Amy's face, her top lip darting up to highlight her brilliant white teeth. 'Thanks to you, I'm being allowed into the inner sanctum for the first time.' Her eyes sparkled like a supernova. 'This is a great honour for me.'

The metal box continued to fall. 'What's the inner sanctum?'

She ran her fingers across her lips and scratched at the dimple in her chin. 'Well, I'm not a hundred per cent sure, though Dr Silk told me it's where all the Foundation's most important work takes place.'

The lift juddered to a halt. Amy opened the door into vivid white light. I had to shield my eyes until my mother's voice drifted across to me.

'I'm sorry, girls; one of the new residents needs a burst of illumination on their body now and then.'

The lights were reduced to normal and I removed my

hand from my face. We were in a large room, as clean as the ones upstairs, but there were no white-uniformed staff here, apart from Dr Silk and my mother, who looked like a research assistant in her long pale coat.

But it wasn't she who made me gasp in amazement. Amy grabbed hold of my arm and stumbled into me, and I didn't blame her. She'd said earlier she wished the supernatural was real.

And now she had that wish.

A small girl, maybe fourteen or fifteen years old, strode towards us. She was covered from head to toe in the most extravagant tattoos; I wasn't sure if she wore any clothes. And then wings unfolded from her back, and she hovered in the air. A teenage boy with horns stood on one side of her, while on the other was a young woman whose hands, out of which great claws grew from her fingers, reached to the ground.

My mother stepped next to them.

'Welcome, Alice, to the community of the supernatural.'

4 CASSIE: DEVASTATION

My vision blurred as the angel dragged me from the cell and into what Gabriel called the Devastation. A howling wind was everywhere, wailing over me and battering my ears, pushing up into my head and thrusting icy tendrils into my brain. The pain forced my face up and my eyes open as my feet brushed against the ground. It was only then I realised the noise wasn't any storm, but the wails of those surrounding me: angels screaming their sorrow and anger at me.

Around me were the remains of destroyed trees and bushes, the earth scorched and shimmering with a sickly dark colour. It stank not of nature burning, but flesh roasting on a spit. The ruins of buildings and dwellings were between the smouldering vegetation, with broken walls and stones scattered everywhere. As the angel dragged me through the wasteland, my feet caught on the bricks and gravel below me; above my dangling head were swirls of mist that wasn't mist, but the cloud forms of the angels. They spun and dived at me, changing their shape and creating large deformed heads with giant teeth that bit and snapped at me.

I did my best to ignore the vicious apparitions, trying to focus on the other beings on either side of me. As well as the wispy angels, there were others like Gabriel in human form; all of them stared at me on this journey, their dark pupils piercing into my heart.

Seraphiel's white eyes peered into me as he pulled me through this desolation.

'How did you find us, child?'

I coughed and spat dirt from my throat. 'I think I took the wrong bus.'

The angel didn't laugh as I wondered if I'd have been better off staying in Valhalla with Michael. Were these his troops? If they were, it wouldn't matter, anyway. Seraphiel kept dragging me for what seemed like an eternity, but was probably only a few minutes. Then he lifted me three feet into the air and threw me into the middle of a circle of stones.

I buried my face in the ground and thought about staying there; until I heard the roar of a crowd and knew things hadn't improved. I rolled on to my back and peered into the sky; there was no blue or white there, no clouds or birds or stars, only black and purple, so it looked like a huge bruise hanging over my head. Every once in a while, misty angels would float over and hiss at me.

All of me ached as I sat up and the smell of blood hit me; it was dark and rotten and sank into my throat. I twisted to the side and threw up a great gush of bile and whatever the last thing I ate was. I wanted to get up and scream, but Seraphiel shoved a bony hand on my forehead and a volcano exploded in my skull. It was as if my body didn't belong to me, each limb burning with acid from the inside.

My legs felt as if they'd been replaced with rubber bands, dangling underneath me as if I was a broken marionette.

The agony was staggering, the worst I'd ever experienced, as the heat invaded every inch of me. My flesh peeled in the fire, strips of me dripped to the floor as I roasted. This continued for an age, his fingers on my head until the pain subsided and I was elsewhere; no, not somewhere else, but seeing something else: Seraphiel showed me what had happened during Heaven's War.

In the clouds of a golden sky stood Michael, the Prince of Heaven's armies, in the middle of a great battle he was waging against terrible forces. Around him, angels fought angels; wings were ripped to the ground and heavenly flesh burned as both sides tore into each other. Michael hollered a huge cry, holding a glimmering spear aloft as a giant dragon attacked him. He plunged the tip of his weapon into its side while its vast teeth bit into his torso and legs.

His pain surged through me, the jaws of the beast devouring my leg, so I wasn't watching the events anymore, but was part of them. Then, as torture raced through every inch of me, my presence swapped from the archangel to the dragon. Now I could feel the fangs biting into Michael and sense the pleasure the creature got from this.

Then, as my mind switched between agony and ecstasy, I was pulled from the action and back into my body.

The beast fell, dragging down a host of spirits resembling ugly grimacing bats flapping in vain as they tumbled into an abyss. Next to the archangel were other angels protecting the souls of the dead. The dragon rose and changed into Satan, into the Morningstar, and then into Lucy. She had an angel army with her, fighting for the possession of Heaven and human souls.

On the right, one of Michael's angels raised a short

sword above Lucy's head, bringing it down and catching her ear. She screamed and clasped at her wound, with blood dripping everywhere. Angels destroyed angels as the great battle continued and my mind returned to the present.

Seraphiel stood over my rigid frame, while above me were hundreds if not thousands of angels, gazing down at me as if ready to pass judgement. Seraphiel's voice boomed out across the Devastation and my ears trembled as he pointed at me.

'Brothers and sisters, this abomination is a consequence of the First War in Heaven.' Blood dripped from my lips and to the ground. Blood will find blood. 'We have to bring that ancient conflict to an end and stop fighting amongst ourselves. Soon the Creator will return, and Their Will is to start again. We need to decide now whether to help Them.' The angels roared around me. 'But no matter what we choose, the Children of the Nephilim cannot be allowed to live. They are blasphemy and must die.' The racket continued as I wanted to collapse into the cold earth below me. I tried to speak, but nothing came out. My tongue shrivelled inside my mouth and my throat closed up. I didn't know if this was Seraphiel's doing or my body finally shutting down after what I'd been through. Or perhaps it was the accumulation of everything I'd done since, as my father claimed, he'd spirited Alice and me from that hospital sixteen years ago.

As I tried to find relief from the pain, I realised I was in the middle of two sides arguing for and against their God. The clatter of angel voices made my head hurt as they shouted at each other, claiming one side was more righteous than the other. The arguments continued as I lay and regained my strength, staring into the bruised sky and listening to their words.

'The First War in Heaven was because Satan rebelled against God,' Seraphiel said.

This got a lot of the angels banging their fists and beating their wings.

Seraphiel continued. 'Satan was a child defying the Creator, and all because they were jealous of humans.'

But not all the angels agreed with that. One of them broke away from the hive and approached Seraphiel.

'If that was so, then why did so many angels follow the Morningstar into battle?' he shouted.

Seraphiel dismissed him with a wave of the hand. 'You were there, Beelzebub. You know the truth of what happened. You and the rest of Satan's followers are here by my Grace, but I have no tolerance for your lies.'

Beelzebub! I'd thought that was just another name for Satan. As much as my body ached and I was desperate to get out of this place, I had to process what they said. All I cared about was regaining my strength and getting away, but as I listened to the arguments erupting around me, some of it intrigued me. Why would hundreds, if not thousands, of angels stand with Lucy if it was all about a spoilt child spitting their dummy out against a parent? Why were some angels, even now, taking the opposite side to God's plan to redo Creation?

I continued to listen to them. God gave man agency, Seraphiel said, and Satan rebelled against that, supposedly jealous of mankind; funny how this was always about man and mankind. No wonder Lucifer became Lucy at some point.

But why would so many angels be bothered about humanity having free will? If it was all about Satan's pride, why would they care?

Beelzebub continued. 'Yes, Seraphiel, I was there, the

same as you.' He glanced at the other angels, most of whom were now quiet. 'We are part of the lucky few who survived, two who should have learned valuable lessons from that conflict. Yet you and others want to repeat that war.' He held up one hand. 'I think all you and they care about is the blood you will spill in your obsession with controlling the humans.'

The angels roared again, with both sides shouting at each other. Seraphiel quietened them by raising his hands.

'Satan rebelled against God the Creator of us all. The First of the Fallen forced us with them - including you, Beelzebub - when they were thrown out of Heaven. That is the truth of the war, and you and Lucy want to continue that conflict because you know God is returning to us after thousands of years. You and Lucy fear the loss of your power. That is the only reason you crave a new conflict.'

I expected the angels to howl again, but I was surrounded by deathly silence instead. But the tension was still in the air and I was glad of that. If a conflict broke out now, perhaps with my help, it might aid me in escaping.

But what about my father? Would I leave him here?

As I was considering that, Beelzebub replied.

'You are the one who lies, Seraphiel. When the Creator spoke of humans and their ascension into Heaven to join the angels, They said certain souls could not be saved. Instead, some would go to other places, terrible realms, to suffer for all of eternity. And this is where the greatest lie of history began.' Beelzebub paused, the air around him surging with what seemed like electricity until I saw that every angel's Grace was burning bright inside them. 'This was the lie that forced Satan to rebel against the Creator. It was not fuelled by jealousy of humans because the opposite is true. Satan said they could save all human souls and laid plans before the Grand Council to achieve this. The Council deliberated and gave its voice to God. So the Devil rose in rebellion against God and was cast down with all the other insurgents.'

The angel voices erupted again and both sides shouted at each other. I sat up as the aching in my body lessened, watching and listening to this debate going back and forth. None of it made any sense. Why wouldn't the Creator be able to save all human souls? Fair enough, some souls aren't worth saving, even if that's what God wanted, but why claim They couldn't save them all? And why would Lucy say they could and know how to do it?

As the pain disappeared through my body, it all seemed to transfer into my skull; my brain felt like it was in a microwave. And then something popped into my head and I stood. No one noticed me standing there staring at them until I coughed loudly.

Seraphiel turned to me.

I smiled at him. 'I'm bored.'

He returned with a grin of his own. 'Your turn will come.' He glanced around at his chattering brethren. 'We'll have the vote, and then get to you.'

'What are you voting on?'

His eyes narrowed so I could hardly see the swirling milky white inside them.

'Haven't you been paying attention, child of blasphemy? We must decide which side we'll be on when God returns: to save the humans or rid the planet of them. We can't do that without remembering how we got here in the first place, and that was so long ago.'

'You don't all support your Creator blindly, then?'

I think when he discovered me in the cell, I was nothing but a sideshow for Seraphiel, but now his eyes glistened in the white as I piqued his interest; or perhaps he was bored with the others talking in circles, like I was.

He scowled at me. 'Do you do everything your parents tell you?'

'I don't have any parents, remember? One of your lot stole me from the hospital and separated me from my twin.'

He laughed, a big throaty squall like a bear about to rip out someone's guts.

'Not all the Heavenly Host are obsessed with the Nephilim, child. You and your sister are a blasphemy against the Creator, and you'll face punishment for that, but you're nothing more than a distraction. The Arcane powers are a myth, believed only by a few conspiracy theorists.'

'Including Michael and Lucy.'

He grinned at me. 'Archangels aren't infallible; only God the Creator has that blessing.'

'So, if that's true and God is infallible, why are you all arguing now?'

He peered through me. 'What?'

'Infallibility means you're never wrong, right? So if God wants to remove Their creations from the planet, to wipe the world clean and start again, then that's what you should all agree on. There's no argument to be had here.' I watched the lines creep below his eyes. 'Unless something else is going on?'

'You are truly a blasphemous child.' He loomed over me.

'I listened to all the discussions and arguments, and it was all so contradictory. I understand why people get confused on Earth, with all the different translations and interpretations, and it's been so many years since the War in Heaven happened.' I twisted my head around the arena to look at them all. 'But you lot were there; you should know the truth. Perhaps it's an old age thing.' Seraphiel and Beelzebub stared at me as I sensed every angel gazing in my direction. 'I can tell you my interpretation of it, if you'd like.'

I felt great. The throbbing had ceased in my skull and there was movement in my body again. My Arcane abilities hadn't returned, but I appeared fit and healthy for the first time in ages.

Then Seraphiel lifted his arm and whacked me in the head. I went flying across the ground and hit the bottom of a tree. A star exploded inside my skull and spat thick lava all over my brain. I rubbed at my jaw as he quietened the crowd and spoke to them.

'Brothers and sisters, we'll vote on this matter later. First, we must start the trial.' He gazed at me.

'What?' I said.

'Now it's the trial of Cassandra Kane. And the only verdict will be death.'

5 ALICE: GENETICS

Amy gripped my hand so hard, I thought she'd break my fingers. I prised her off and spoke to my mother. 'What's this?'

The winged girl flew away and her companions ran after her.

'This is the real reason I created the Foundation.' She turned and bade me follow. I nodded to Amy, concerned about the fear in her eyes. We strode together towards my mother and Dr Silk.

'You collect supernatural creatures?' My mind returned to the Nexus and how Dr Rivers had imprisoned all those unfortunate beings between damp walls deep below the island of Lindisfarne.

'We don't collect them, Alice.' There was disappointment in her voice. 'We rescue them from the predators inhabiting this planet. We protect them, give them homes, find them jobs, and make sure they can exist in a world which hates them.'

Amy stumbled ahead of me. 'This is amazing.' Her eyes

fixed on the horned boy. I couldn't take my gaze from the girl with the extended arms and claws.

'It's all genetics?'

Amy turned to me. 'What do you mean?'

My mother sat at the table while Dr Silk spoke to the winged girl as she hovered in the air.

'Yes, Alice, what do you mean?'

I took hold of Amy's arm. 'Supernatural creatures exist.' She glanced from the horned boy to me. 'All the things you've read about in books or seen in movies which you thought were fictional are real: vampires, werewolves, angels, demons.' I watched her face shiver in amazement or fear. 'Apparently, even God exists, and They created these beings, but I think it's all down to evolution and genetics.'

My mother smiled at me. 'This is fascinating; go on, Alice.' Her gaze bored into me and my blood started to simmer. Neither she nor Dr Silk seemed concerned they'd thrust Amy into a new and terrifying realm.

'There's more to life than what we've been told; I accept that now.' It had been a bitter pill to swallow at first, but I'd washed it down my throat, eventually. 'But I think even the supernatural world follows similar rules to those of the natural one.'

Dr Silk sat next to my mother, appearing to hang on my every word. 'Science and the supernatural go hand in hand.' He beamed at me. 'I've tried telling this to many of my colleagues, but they only laugh.'

'Yes, well, that may be true, but the adjective form of supernatural describes anything that pertains to or is caused by something the laws of nature can't explain. So your colleagues don't believe you because they haven't experienced the truth with their own eyes.'

'And what truth is that, daughter of mine?'

Her glare grated on me and I didn't know why. 'All life on Earth is connected and related to each other. This diversity of existence is a product of modifications of populations by natural selection, where some traits are favoured in an environment over others.'

Dr Silk clasped his hands together. 'You're talking about Darwin's theory of evolution.'

'I am, but Darwin was theorising about the natural world, not the supernatural. Nevertheless, I believe his ideas still apply. It's all to do with blood and genetics, reproduction and modifications.' I was enjoying this. I'd stopped being an academic and scientist not long after Cassie had drawn me into her universe. As much as I loved my long-lost identical twin sister, I enjoyed the educational life I'd had before: the one I'd abandoned to reunite with my family.

'How do you propose this supernatural evolution began if it has nothing to do with God the Creator?' My mother appeared keen to hear me out, but it also felt like she was testing me.

'All current living organisms on Earth share a common genetic heritage, a mutual ancestor.' My studies of Darwin were the first things I'd read and marvelled at.

Dr Silk scratched at his nose. 'Darwin said it's likely all organic beings which have ever lived on this planet have descended from a single primordial form, into which life first breathed.'

'Yes, and I agree; and now, after my recent experiences, I'd theorise supernatural creatures follow the same pattern. In humanity's dim and distant past, the natural and the supernatural must have co-existed side by side. Maybe it was troublesome and a violent co-existence, and this is where all tales, myths and legends originate from, but at some point, the supernatural shrank back into the shadows, and reason and logic took over the human world. But I'd guess this period has only been for a few hundred years, and even now, there are still many stories of the fantastical seeping into civilisation.'

I waited for my mother to respond, but it was Amy who spoke.

'What if it's not Darwinism, but panspermia?'

I stared at her with newfound fascination. 'Panspermia? The belief that certain aspects of life and evolution may have developed due to "seeds" of matter that came to Earth from other planets?'

Amy nodded. 'Wouldn't seeds from outer space be just another way of saying God created all life?'

My mother looked at her as if she was some stupid kid while Dr Silk shook his head. But I had an idea where Amy had got this notion from.

'You're thinking about octopuses, aren't you?'

Amy grinned at me. 'I read a scientific paper about it. According to evolution, animals with the most adaptive characteristics will probably survive and reproduce more than disadvantaged animals, passing down these traits, which change and refine over time, creating evolution as we know it. But the octopus is a little different.

'The main characteristics we associate with octopuses - their giant non-centralised brain, camouflage abilities and flexible bodies - all appeared on the evolutionary scene quite suddenly. Before then, the octopuses' ancestors looked very different because they were shelled.

'One of the earliest fossils from this era shows a sudden divergence from this shelled creature to a non-shelled one. And there's no evolutionary explanation for it. Which is why some scientists have theorised their ancestral eggs might have come to Earth in icy bolides several hundred million years ago.'

Dr Silk clapped his hands. 'You're an intelligent young woman, Amy, which is why Mary and I asked you down here today, but sometimes I think you let your imagination run wild.'

His tone was condescending and it annoyed me. 'I'm not saying I agree with her, but why is what she said any different from my theory? That element must have come from somewhere if the natural and the supernatural originated from the same evolutionary strand. And outer space is as good a place as any.'

The winged girl lowered herself to the ground to listen to me. The horned boy and clawed girl also stared at me as I spoke.

My mother pointed at the three of them. 'Where do you think they fit into this theory of yours?'

I wouldn't admit I hadn't thought the whole thing through, but I considered her question. 'Given enough time and accumulated changes, natural selection can create entirely new species, known as macroevolution. It can turn dinosaurs into birds, amphibious mammals into whales, and apes' ancestors into humans.' I looked at the three supernatural teenagers. 'I think with a proper comprehensive study and archiving of each supernatural type, we could link every creature back to a starting point.' I glanced at the winged girl. 'For example, is there a connection between each living thing with wings? Is there an association between shapeshifters and werewolves?' I smiled at Amy. 'An octopus can change its shape and appearance. Studies have proved it isn't a reflex or a response, but a calculated transformation.' After an age of running and fighting, I had an entire world of scientific learning about the supernatural opening up to me. Perhaps this was my destiny.

My mother tried to throw a spanner in the works. 'What about God; angels and demons; Heaven and Hell?'

'Don't forget Limbo and Purgatory,' I said.

I finally got a look of surprise from her. 'You've been to those places?'

'A ghost ship and its crew took us to Purgatory, while Cassie and I went to Limbo to search for the entrance to Hell to find you.'

Even from where I stood, I saw the tear in her eye. 'You are my beautiful daughters, my children of the Arcane.'

I tried not to let thoughts of Cassie distract me. 'I've yet to meet anyone or anything that has met God, but angels may well be at the start of the evolutionary supernatural chain, and the Devil created demons.'

Silence engulfed the room. Amy and the teenagers were crestfallen; even my mother and Dr Silk appeared mortified.

She got up from the table.

'How do you know this, Alice?'

'After Satan's Fall from Grace, Lucy wanted to create her children. She experimented with her blood on several creatures until she fashioned the demon virus. This virus infects humans and created demons who Lucy controls.' The incredulous looks on all their faces amused me. 'Therefore, everything comes from the blood.' I remembered Lucy's dried blood on my jacket.

My mother hadn't forgotten about it either.

'That's how you teleported us from Buckingham Palace: you drank Lucy's blood to kick start your abilities?'

I didn't answer her question, but gave her my own. 'As one of the Nephilim, do you have special powers?'

She walked from the table and towards me. 'My

heritage is half human and half archangel; the angel blood strengthens me to be greater than most other creatures, but I can't do what you can.'

It was time to face the truth about my parents. 'Is this because my father was an archangel?'

She flinched at the question. I assumed the reaction was because he'd betrayed her, and abandoned Cassie and me. Her voice trembled as she spoke.

'According to many, your lineage is an abomination: the Nephilim and archangel child that should never have been. That's what the supernatural world thinks of you and your sister.'

'We are the Arcane.'

'Yes, and no one knows what potential lies inside you.'

'The potential for either good or bad?'

'That's what some say. Your abilities, derived from the archangels and expanded by the mixture of Nephilim blood, will manifest as you get older and mature into adulthood.' A grave look overtook her face. 'But it would appear drinking specific types of blood can spark an early onset of your gifts. Is it only angel blood which does this?'

I hesitated with my reply. 'Demon blood has the same effect, though it acts as a poison to me.'

Dr Silk leapt from the table and startled Amy even more than she already was. 'This is marvellous.' He turned to my mother. 'This confirms all we spoke about.'

She glared at him. 'That's enough for now, Julius; let's show the girls the rest of the facility here.'

He wiped a slither of sweat from his forehead, even though there was no heat in the room. 'Of course, Mary, of course.' He looked away from her to his employee. 'Come, Amy; this is all part of your Foundation training.'

We marched together, my mother at the far end of the

line from me, as Dr Silk took us through the living quarters for the rescued supernaturals. He spoke about how the organisation had integrated several supernaturals into the human world in my mother's absence.

An aroma of fresh bread drifted down the corridor. We continued and entered a dining area with a kitchen. A tall man, maybe seven feet in height, placed food on an enormous table.

Amy whispered into my ear. 'I told you there'd be grub.'

The teenagers scampered to the table while Dr Silk and my mother engaged in a heated conversation on the other side of the room. I took Amy by the arm.

'Are you okay with what you've seen and heard here?'

Her eyes beamed with excitement and her lips trembled. 'I have to admit it was a bit of a shock at first. I thought it might be a practical joke or a test, but, well, once you spoke, I knew it was all true and everything would be okay.'

'It's a whole new world for you.'

She grabbed my hand. 'It is and it isn't.'

'What do you mean?'

'I've seen some strange things in Leeds at night, when I thought I was drunk or high and, this answers some of my questions.'

She let go of me as my mother approached.

'So, what do you think, girls? Are you happy to fit in with what we're doing here?'

Amy was ecstatic. 'Absolutely, err...'

'Call me Mary.'

'Oh yes, Mary. I can't wait to start.'

The smell of the food reminded me I hadn't eaten since the train. 'Start on what?'

Dr Silk handed us both the smallest phones I'd ever seen. 'You should tell them, Mary; it's your project.'

My mother threw her arms around Amy and me. 'You two girls will help the Foundation rescue the oppressed supernatural beings in this city.' She squeezed us. 'And then we'll do it for the rest of the country.'

She beamed at me as a gnarled knot gripped my gut.

6 CASSIE: THE TRIAL

Screaming covered the sky, but the ringing inside my ears wasn't because of that; a group of warring angels was about to put me on trial, and it looked like they'd already decided on the verdict.

Seraphiel waved towards the swirling angels to stop circling above as the crowd descended into a hush, and they flew away. They dragged Gabriel into the middle with me, unchained and dumped at my feet. I bent to help him up, taking him by the arm. He was nothing but skin and bones underneath those rags. As I lifted him, I got a better look at his severed wings, smelling the dried blood on the bits sticking out of his back.

'You need someone to speak for you during the trial, Cassie.' I wondered if he was volunteering; he must have thought the same thing. 'Alas, it cannot be me.'

I peered into his face, tried to stare beyond the withered, unruly beard and the sunken cheekbones; deep into those eyes which had given up on life. And that's where I saw it: the resemblance to Alice, and hence to me. There was no doubting he was my father.

Blood will find blood.

I held his hand and smiled at him. All we had to do was get away, return to Earth, and find Alice and my mother. That thought spun around inside my head as I scanned those surrounding me in a great circle, hundreds of angels ready to put me to death. Seraphiel and Beelzebub had forgotten their argument and were focused on me. The other angels shouted and shrieked, talked and chatted, and I guessed all of them only had one thing on their minds: my execution.

I pulled my father close to me as Seraphiel hushed those who were to be my judge and jury. His voice was loud enough to travel across the whole of the Devastation.

'Now begins the Trial of Cassandra Kane, also known as a Child of the Nephilim.' He let the whispers turn into a murmur. Maybe he was advising any latecomers or those who didn't know who I was, which seemed highly unlikely in the horde who stared at me.

I released Gabriel and tapped Seraphiel on the arm.

'Do I get someone to defend me?'

He rubbed his hands together, apparently pleased I'd spoken up.

'Your chance will come later, abomination.' I hadn't heard that insult since my second foster home. 'One advocate can speak for you and one alone.'

I scanned the expectant crowd, looked up at the gaseous angels hovering above me before turning to Gabriel.

'You better make notes, Father.'

It was strange saying that word aloud and it made us both smile. And then Seraphiel wiped that smile away.

'Humans were God's chosen creations on Earth, while the angels were his favourites in Heaven. When people multiplied and daughters were born to them, the sons of

God saw that they were fair. And when the angels, the sons of Heaven, beheld them, they became enamoured of them, saying to each other, "Come, let us select for ourselves wives from the progeny of men, and let us beget children."

'And these children were the Nephilim. God was so offended by these creatures, the Creator sent the Great Flood to cleanse the Earth of such blasphemy. Then, with the planet washed clean, God granted some disembodied spirits of the Nephilim the chance to remain after the flood, to lead humans astray until the Final Judgement, to test humanity in its worship of God the Creator.

'And now the Final Judgement is upon us. All that remain of the Nephilim are its progeny, Alice and Cassandra. Some angels want to use them to defeat God's plans, and others wish to worship them; neither of these can happen with such blasphemous children. It is up to us, brothers and sisters, to wipe these girls from existence; and that starts now.'

The angels in human form stamped their feet, beat their wings, and raised their fists. They roared and chanted as one; there was no division now, no argument over what my fate would be. The gaseous angels swooped and swirled across the bruised sky like excitable snakes ready to feast on some unsuspecting prey. Then Seraphiel turned to me.

'Do you have any last words?'

So much for having an advocate. My father had his head in his hands as I stepped forward.

'Angels of the Devastation, you have nothing to fear from me.' My voice was a whisper compared to Seraphiel's and I wondered if any of them could hear me. The chorus of boos and insults answered that.

'I am an outsider, but you see me as impure.' I thought of blood finding blood. 'I am a daughter, but you see me as an abomination.' I glanced at Gabriel. 'I am a sister, but you see me as a monster.' I pictured Alice and me together again. 'You accuse me of crimes I haven't committed. You fear me because I'm different from you, different from everyone else but one other: my sister.' The hatred was so intense it was like a wave hurtling towards me. 'The very sight of me makes you sick because it reminds you of God's pettiness, of God's jealousy.'

They roared their outrage, howling and rising in the air as their wings beat at a frantic pace. I think most of them were on the brink of attacking me at any second. So I gave them more ammunition for that.

'Imagine, the Creator of All Things spitting Their dummy out because angels and humans created children, the Nephilim. Imagine being so vengeful of this, They sent the Great Flood to kill most creatures on the planet. And now the Creator is returning to finish what They started.' I moved to Gabriel and took his hand. 'Imagine being a parent so damaged, with such feelings of inferiority, you want to kill your children.' I watched the misty angels swirling around me, every one of them vibrating a dark red. 'So many of you hate humans, yet here you are, ready to pass judgement on me while you exist inside human bodies: bodies which were given to you willingly, because of human love for angels; because of human love for you.'

I could have sworn there were a few murmuring voices of dissent within their ranks, but a look at Seraphiel told me it wouldn't make any difference: they'd made their decision long before I'd spoken. But I continued.

'You are as envious as your Creator, with minds corrupted by jealousy of humans. You might have that light inside you, but you have become immune to true Grace. Without a physical human form, you are ephemeral, a transient blip in the world's history. You are nothing without the humans you want to destroy. Satan was right all along.'

Their disapproval turned into a racket, with every angel leaping up and gesturing towards me.

Seraphiel scowled. 'You've gone too far now, abomination. It is not your place to speak for the First of the Fallen. The angels will tear you apart for your blasphemy.'

I ignored the venom in his words. 'You need humans to survive. I believe that's what Satan put to your so-called Great Council. Once God destroys all living things, what will you do then?'

Seraphiel raised his arm, ready to strike me down before any of the others could.

'I told you not to speak for the Morningstar, abomination; it's not your right to do so.'

'And neither is it yours, Seraphiel.'

A flash of brilliant white light followed her voice. She was behind me, so I didn't get the full force of it, but all the angels did; even the gaseous ones were blasted from the sky and driven far beyond the baying crowd. I turned, and Lucy gave me a slight bow. She was dressed as a Victorian gentleman, wearing a high narrow-brimmed hat, long-tailed coat, and tight trousers. Her shirt was a shocking purple and fluffed up like the cheeks of a pufferfish. She took out an ornate pocket watch and checked the time.

'What are you doing here, Lucy?' It was my father who spoke.

'Nice to see you, Gabriel. It's been far too long. When was the last time we snatched a sneaky kiss amongst the shadows?' She slipped the watch into her jacket. My father said nothing, appearing to turn a faint shade of pink beneath that beard. 'Silly me, we shouldn't talk about these things in front of the children, should we?'

'What did you do with my sister?' It was all I could do not to throw myself at her. Instead, I flexed my fingers in anticipation of getting them around her scrawny neck.

Lucy removed a handkerchief from her top pocket and used it to dab at her cheeks.

'I'm afraid Alice is in trouble, Cassie; in a lot of trouble. And I can't help her.' She smirked at me. 'So I came here to help you instead.' The crowd of angels were regaining their positions. 'I mean, I owe you for what you did in that bunker with the president. I never got the chance to thank you for that, so here I am now. And I hear you've recently given my brother another bloody nose.' She clasped her hands together, and then clapped. 'Bravo, Cassie, bravo.'

'Can you get my father and me out of here?'

She shook her head as the angel discord started again.

'I'm afraid not; there are many rules regarding angel trials, and nobody can break them, not even me.'

My ribs hurt with laughter. 'You're telling me the Queen of Lies, the Daughter of Deception, plays by the rules?'

A mobile phone appeared in her hand from nowhere. 'Oh, that's a good one, Daughter of Deception. I've never heard of that before. Just let me make a note of it.'

'There is no place for you here, Morningstar,' Seraphiel said.

She waved the phone at him. 'Oh, don't worry, my old friend. I'm not here for me, but her. I'm Cassie's advocate.'

'You will speak for the blasphemous child?'

Lucy leant towards me. 'He's got a right potty mouth, hasn't he?'

'It's not allowed, Morningstar.'

The mobile disappeared from Lucy's hand, exchanged for a book. She flicked through the pages.

'Would you like me to show you the ruling? I could have the whole trial dismissed if you refute the rules. You know this.'

Seraphiel stood there and seethed while the angels hummed and boiled. The gaseous ones had returned, but they kept their distance, apparently fearful of Lucy. Seraphiel turned to the crowd while I moved towards the Devil.

'You lied about the training; it was no such thing. You fed me your blood to bring out my abilities, didn't you?'

She shrugged. 'I cannot tell a lie, so alas, all you say is true.'

'And what about Alice? You could have done the same with her; why did you make her think she was a failure?'

'It wasn't the right time for your sister, Cassie; you're the mature one.'

I didn't believe her for a second. 'So, you'll speak on my behalf and save me from execution.'

She winked at me. 'Well, I'll try, but no promises.'

Gabriel grabbed me as she switched her attention to the crowd. 'You can't trust her.'

It wasn't news to me, but I only smiled at him in return.

Lucy strode forward and spoke to the angels. 'Brothers and sisters, listen to me.' A thousand voices turned into a hush. 'A long time ago, I came to you and said I could save every human soul. I stand before you now and say I know how to save every human life, how to save every living thing in existence.' She glanced at me. 'The only way to stop God's senseless slaughter is to put our faith in this girl and her sister.'

The uproar returned when she'd finished. Staring into the multitude of angels and listening to their voices, I heard even more hatred than before. I went to the Morningstar.

'Well, that was brilliant.' I gave her a mock clap. 'I didn't think things could get any worse, but they have. And it's all thanks to you.'

Did she come here to make sure the angels killed me?

She scratched her head and looked at her pocket watch again. 'I have a date somewhere else, so I must love you and leave you.' I lunged at her, but she stepped to the side.

'It's time to kill the abomination and its father,' Seraphiel shouted above the baying of the crowd.

I glared at Lucy. She had one last thing to say to me before she disappeared.

'Your destiny is in your hands, Cassandra Arcane.'

7 ALICE: AMY

I pulled away from my mother and dropped the phone on the table.

'What about going to America and finding Cassie?' A cocktail of anger and hunger swirled inside me. The teenagers dipped into the food, but continued to sneak glances our way. Dr Silk stood there explaining something to Amy, but it wasn't difficult to notice their attention was also on the conversation between my mother and me.

She wore her kindness in her eyes and smile. 'We'll get to America soon enough, Alice. Julius has already spoken to his contacts across the Atlantic. When we know where Cassie is, we'll be straight there, don't you worry.' She placed a calming hand on my shoulder. 'The Foundation has plenty of resources to use. I only thought you might like to keep busy while we wait. But if you want to stay inside...'

She let the sentence drift away.

'No, you're right; it's just that, well, the impatience is bugging me.' I glanced at the teenagers pretending not to watch us. 'It would be good to observe the work here and partake in Foundation activities helping others.'

'That's great, Alice.' She pulled me close. 'Now maybe you should get something to eat before heading out later.'

The winged girl moved over so I could sit next to her. There was rice with a potato and cauliflower curry on the table. She smiled and served me at the same time.

'Thanks,' I said to her before returning my focus to my mother. 'What's happening tonight?' I shovelled the food into my mouth, enjoying the spices slipping between my lips.

Dr Silk sat opposite and answered my question. 'One of our teenage witches disappeared from a club last night, and we believe a local drugs gang is holding her captive.' He showed me a photo on his phone of a dark-haired girl with piercing blue eyes.

There was a garlic nan bread next to me, so I tore a slice off and dipped it into the curry. I bit into it and spoke at the same time.

'I thought all magic came from artefacts and not spells.' That's what Kai the Warwitch had told me back at the Impossible Palace inside Whitby Abbey.

Mother joined us at the table. 'That's only for those not with the power of witchcraft in their blood. Natural born witches, and warlocks, can conjure up all kinds of magic. Through the ages, few have lived beyond their teenage years, especially the girls. Julius told me we've had two here in the Foundation for about six months, cousins who fled their war-torn country and are learning English, getting ready to assimilate into the wider community. But it was Malika's eighteenth birthday yesterday, and she went to a concert away from the city centre and hasn't been seen since.'

'What makes you think a drug gang would have her?'

Dr Silk stood, a hardened expression stretched across his face. 'Do you know what alchemy was?'

I'd read a lot of books, so I knew something about it. I reached into my memory and a passage in a dusty volume I'd flicked through a long time ago.

'It was chemistry and speculative philosophy practised in the Middle Ages and the Renaissance, concerned with discovering methods for transmuting baser metals into gold, with finding a universal solvent and an elixir of life. It's been debunked as an entire pot of nonsense.'

Even as I said that, the girl fluttered her wings next to me, and I wondered if anything could be described as nonsense anymore.

Julius Silk grinned at me. 'Alchemy was based on the belief there are four basic elements in nature: air, fire, water and earth. Natural magic has the same basis. Malika's chief talent is being able to turn one chemical substance into another. You can see how that would be attractive to certain individuals and groups.'

I was sure it would tempt many on the planet, but it would be manna from Heaven for drug dealers. 'So, they discovered what she could do and have spirited her away to a drug-making factory in the city?'

'That's what our sources told us, but these people won't keep her in Leeds for long. They'll have her out of the country and whisked off to a more profitable bit of the world sooner rather than later. That's why we need you and Amy in that club tonight.'

Amy spat out the onion bhaji she was eating. 'Me? Why do you want me to go?'

'Because you know the area, Amy, and now you've been introduced to the real work of the Foundation, you have to be immersed in it if you want to continue with us.' Silk smiled at her, but it was impossible to miss the veiled threat in his voice.

I stared at my mother. 'Why should I go? I've only been in the city a few hours.'

Not that I didn't want to do it. Anything was preferable to having Cassie's situation on my mind, but I wondered why these adults trusted two young people for such a critical operation.

'You're a warrior, Alice,' my mother said. 'I've seen it with my own eyes. And from what Julius has told me about the Foundation in my forced absence, there's no one here capable of handling something like this.'

Dr Silk held up his hands in mock capitulation. 'It's true; we're all scientists and academics here. We couldn't infiltrate a criminal gang and retrieve Malika, and we can't go to the police.'

Mother continued. 'We've spread a rumour around the area where the club is that another witch will be there tonight. The description they have is of you, Alice.'

What she said should have surprised me, her using me without my knowledge or say so, but it didn't; there was still so much about her I didn't know. But the look of fear in Amy's eyes meant it wasn't sitting well with her. I guessed she had to decide whether to stay with the Foundation or not. She peered at me, and I gave her my best comforting smile.

She turned to her bosses. 'Okay, I'll do it. When do we start?'

I finished my food and pulled her up with me. 'There's no time like the present.' I removed the mini mobile I had been given earlier from my pocket. 'What do we use these for?' I was keen to get my phone and call Medusa to see how she was since I hadn't heard from her in a few days.

Mother put her arms around Amy and me again. 'I'll tell you all about them on the way out, girls.'

As we headed to the lift, the winged girl gave me a nervous grin.

Twenty minutes later, we were outside in the darkening gloom and cold of the Leeds night. Amy had changed into a set of clothes which were the mirror image of what she'd got for me. I'd retrieved my jacket from the room, but left my phone to continue charging. Amy stared at the Foundation device in her hand. There were only a few numbers on them: each other's, Dr Silk's, and my mother's. They also contained a recent photo of Malika.

I swiped mine into life and peered at the image of our missing witch. Her complexion and hair were the same shade of beautiful brown, her face with cerulean blue eyes sparkling in the photograph. She appeared older than eighteen, but I guessed that was the way with many teenage girls now. I remembered how old I'd looked when I'd forced myself to stare into the mirror, seeing a lifetime of experience etched in my face that wasn't there a few weeks ago. Then I slipped the phone into my pocket.

'How long will it take to walk to this club, Amy?'

Amy blinked as if I'd asked her to run a marathon in high heels. She resembled a pop-eyed toy from one of those claw machines at the funfair.

'Shouldn't we get a taxi?'

'Is it far from here?'

'It's about a twenty-minute stroll that way.' She pointed to our right.

I strode in that direction. 'Come on then. The exercise will get the blood flowing.'

She struggled to keep up with me at first, so I slowed my

pace a little. Her voice wobbled with a mixture of anticipation and tension as she spoke.

'Have you done this before?'

We stepped past a group of homeless people huddled in doorways. The building next to them was a church advertising a nightly Food Bank between six and eight. It had just closed.

'What do you mean?'

Amy brushed a stray hair from her eyes. 'Have you had many dealings with the supernatural?'

I grinned. 'I thought you were talking about meeting drug gangs.'

'There is that.' It was the first time she'd smiled since we'd left the Foundation. 'But I meant fighting to save innocent people.'

'I'm not sure if supernatural creatures are classed as people, but I'll stick up for every living thing that faces oppression. I promise we'll find this teenager and get her back.' Since meeting Cassie and stepping into the supernatural world, I'd let so many down, and each of them weighed upon my mind. Helping this missing girl might just ease my guilty conscience a little.

The wind blew my jacket into my clean clothes, a shred of light bouncing off the moon and revealing the dried blood close to my chest. Would I use it if I had to? Surely I wouldn't need it to deal with a few drug dealers.

I laughed at myself inside my head. A month ago, I'd have run away at the thought of even seeing someone taking drugs, never mind coming into contact with a dealer. Yet, look at me now, striding through this unknown city as if I owned it.

Cars and trucks whizzed by on the road as Amy spoke. 'Is it true what your mother..., what Mary said earlier?'

A group of kids cycled past us, their hoods pulled up to cover their faces, but not enough to block out the whistles they sent our way.

'Everything you heard in there was the truth. My mother is the last of the Nephilim. I never met my father, but apparently, he was an archangel. My twin sister Cassie and I are the Children of the Nephilim, also called the Arcane.'

Amy turned right as she listened, leading out of the industrial area into residential housing, late-night shops and the odd bar and pub.

'Do you have powers?'

It was an excellent question. There was no point in lying to her. 'I've been told many times Cassie and I will develop special abilities as we get older, but they can be brought out sometimes with the right push.'

People shuffled in and out of buildings as we continued. 'What does that mean?'

We stepped across the road and dodged a scruffy dog barking at something only it could see. 'Both angel and demon blood will spark my heritage into early action. Even vampire blood can work.' Amy looked horrified as she listened. 'But demon blood is poison to me. If I take a little, I'll get sick; too much of it, and I'll die.'

Street lights flickered above us as we passed. 'It sounds like taking hard drugs.'

She turned left and I followed. There were many shops and a pub up ahead. 'You're not wrong.'

'The club is next to the pub.' She stopped a few yards away from it. 'How old are you?'

'Sixteen.'

'You should get in, but you won't be able to drink any alcohol.'

'I don't want to. How old are you?'

'I'm twenty-one. What's the plan when we get inside?'

I dragged her into the shadows. 'You're not coming with me.'

'What... why?'

'It's too dangerous, Amy. Your only job was to get me here. I'll deal with it now.'

She puffed her cheeks out at me. 'Could you be any more patronising?'

'Eh?' It wasn't the response I expected.

'You may be the expert on the supernatural, but I've been around drug users and dealers for most of my life. I grew up in a family riddled with them. My mother and father weren't great parents, so I went to live with my aunt and uncle when I was ten. They worked their fingers to the bone to keep me and my cousins fed, clothed and with a roof over our heads. But where we lived was still full of scumbags, and there wasn't a day when I didn't come into contact with stuff no kid should ever have to.' She nodded at the club. 'I know more about what's in there than you.'

If it had been lighter, I'm sure I'd have seen the steam coming from her ears. She stormed away from me and headed for the venue. I'd assumed she was putting on a brave front regarding her introduction to the world of the supernatural, but perhaps she was tougher than she looked.

I removed the phone from my pocket and rechecked the photo of Malika. It was unlikely the girl would be in the club. Amy didn't understand that I needed this drug gang to take me to where they had Malika. And that meant things wouldn't be pretty.

And people would get hurt.

8 CASSIE: THE FIGHT

Seraphiel lunged at me. I was too slow to do anything, but Gabriel got between us and took the full force of the blow. He fell to the ground and cracked his head.

I ran to him. 'Father, are you okay?'

He appeared shaken, but not too hurt. 'I'm fine as long as I'm with you.' I helped him up, and we turned to stare at the descending horde.

So this was how it ended, torn apart by a thousand crazed angels in a devastated garden on the edge of Heaven. How ironic it was to find my father finally, but then lose him again so soon afterwards. It was the same as when Alice and I had gone back in time to see our mother in that hospital bed just after she'd given birth to us. I was only with her for a moment before losing her, and now she was Dracula's captive.

But I hoped she was alive. And Alice.

It didn't look too good for my father and me.

Seraphiel held up his spear to the angels gathering behind him. 'It's my duty to rid God's creation of the blasphemous abomination, for I am the Angel of Silence.'

He towered over me, raised to over seven feet, with enormous golden wings spread out from his back. Lightning jumped from the spear and sparkled around him. Seraphiel flicked his head and stared straight into the bruised sky; his lips moved as he spoke silently to something only he could see.

I kept hold of Gabriel and thought of how much I hated Lucy for betraying me again. She must have only come here to torment me, to tease me with the chance of escaping the Devastation. And she'd made it worse by saying Alice was in trouble and needed my help. And then I remembered what she'd said.

Your destiny is in your hands, Cassandra Arcane.

The angels' hate spread through the air as I repeated those words.

Your destiny is in your hands, Cassandra Arcane.

My father held my waist. I peered at my fingers as I waited for Seraphiel to attack. Would Lucy have travelled here just to make sure I died? I didn't think so; she'd had ample opportunities to kill me after I stumbled out of that bunker in America. She needed me, in her twisted way, to satisfy whatever plans she had. She must have been telling me something in her own warped, cryptic fashion.

Gabriel pulled me closer as I gazed at my hand, looking through the dirt and the damp from the prison walls and the ground and settling on the thick red substance under my nails. I put my finger to my lips and tasted it: it was dried blood.

Pandora's blood.

My father pushed his face into mine. 'I need to tell you something about your mother, Cassie. You must know this before we die.'

His words hardly registered with me as I watched Seraphiel spin the spear in a circular shape until the lightning around his head connected to the weapon. The angels roared in anticipation near him. He matched the frantic movement of the spear to their howls of murder, and it came to me in a blinding flash; only it didn't since it appeared to move in slow motion. The murderous cacophony from the mob disappeared and the only thing I heard was the beating of my heart.

Then that tiny drop of dried Pandora blood sparked the return of the Arcane.

Seraphiel's spear was an inch from my face when I teleported Gabriel and me three feet away; it was all I could do with such a slight amount of fuel. Seraphiel gazed at me in amazement as the first wave of angels paused in surprise. My ears buzzed and my fingers trembled. A blurred mist hovered in front of my eyes as the noise in my head increased.

But all was silent around me as a thousand angels glared in my direction. Then Seraphiel and Beelzebub roared at their followers, and I guessed the division of angels was over. They had a mutual enemy now.

I thrust a hand into my mouth and sucked on the blood of the woman the angels had created millennia ago. It was dry and tasted of rusted copper, but it worked; a dozen angels flew at me with their swords brandished, but it took only one flick of my mind to send them flying backwards and straight into the second wave.

They crashed together like a sonic boom as my skull throbbed. A tear slid from my eye, and when I rubbed at it, my finger came away red.

'How are you doing this, abomination?' Fear dripped from Seraphiel's voice.

I felt both terrible and fabulous, with a continuous ache

spreading through me while euphoria pulsed from every muscle and sinew. But I didn't know how long Pandora's blood would last. Retreat seemed to be the best option.

I was about to teleport both of us out of there when a spear pierced my shoulder from behind.

'Cassandra!' Gabriel shouted as I stumbled from him and screamed. I fell forward as pain sped through me. I landed on my other side. As I did so, the weapon withdrew from my body and returned to the angel who had thrown it.

Seraphiel looked more annoyed than I was. 'The privilege is mine, Metatron, not yours.'

'Yet, you weren't doing a very good job of it, brother,' Metatron said.

The others had lost interest in me to watch this little spat. I was happy for them to continue to argue as my blood absorbed Pandora's and the pain disappeared. I turned to find Gabriel, but he wasn't there. It was only when I glanced up that I saw him being carried away by two angels in their gaseous form.

Metatron and Seraphiel glared at each other as I teleported, appearing near Gabriel and throwing a punch at the closer angel. Those below me shouted while my fist caught nothing, and I fell through the gassy creature. It let out what I assumed was a laugh, but sounded like fingernails dragged over a chalkboard. As I covered my ears, I kept on falling, heading towards those waiting for me. It took me a second to remember I could fly.

My mind focused on that as I stopped my descent and rose upwards. I flew towards the angels abducting my father, grabbing hold of Gabriel's legs to haul him away, but somehow, even as gas, they were stronger than me. I pulled with all my Arcane strength, but it was futile. I let go and hovered there, watching them taunting me with gaseous arms stretching at me and waving smoky fingers in my face. I glanced down to see Seraphiel staring at me twenty feet below.

'You can die up there or down here; it's your choice, abomination child.' His wings had grown to twice his size and I wondered if they were like a peacock's, more for show than flight.

Then I returned to my father's ordeal. How could I get him from the gaseous angels if I couldn't touch them and they were stronger than me? And how long would Pandora's blood keep me powered up? I thought of teleporting and leaving him. If I couldn't help Gabriel, then there was no point in hanging around.

But he was my father. So whatever his reasons were for sending Alice and me away at birth, I wouldn't leave him to this fate.

I hovered there, letting the angels taunt me, and looked at my hands: one was clear of blood, while on the other, it was only under two of my fingernails. I needed that to teleport us out of this hell, so what could I do?

As the gas held Gabriel and swirled in front of me, I reached into my mind for the telekinesis I'd used to tear the president into pieces. The trigger was there, so I imagined ripping the angels from Gabriel, but nothing happened apart from them unleashing that horrible laugh again. Time was running out, and Seraphiel knew it.

I looked at my hands and thought again about teleporting away and leaving Gabriel, of abandoning my father as he'd done to Alice and me. I stared at him and knew that's what he'd want.

And that's when the solution hit me: telepathy.

I grabbed hold of Gabriel and peered at his captors, and then my mind reached into the closest one. Its thoughts were like its incorporeal body, hazy and intangible, and diffi-cult to grasp. I summoned all my strength and used my consciousness to scream at its mind.

LET HIM GO!

I repeated this as the angel relinquished its grip on Gabriel, drifting away before changing into a swirling, fren-zied tornado. It sped off into the distance, with misty arms twisting and turning and pulling at the space where its face should have been; then it split apart and dissipated into the bruised sky. The other one continued its hold on my father, the shape of its hazy head creating pinpricks of light as eyes that glared at me.

'Go without me,' Gabriel said.

But there was no way I'd leave him after finding him; what happened with my mother wouldn't happen again. I thrust my thoughts into the thing holding him, but it was different this time. Its consciousness was no formless ethe-real shape, but a mind bristling with vivid memories. Inside those memories, angels were tortured and cut open in the war between Michael and Lucy. Rebellion was championed and opposed as thousands of the Heavenly Host battled each other, and, before all this, some angels defied God's wishes and descended to Earth to lie with the daughters of men. This creature's recollections were vile and terrible, and I wanted to pull away from it, desperate to withdraw my consciousness from its cruel presence.

But I couldn't. I endured the revolting thoughts and abhorrent memories and pushed further into its conscious-ness; my mind lashed out with imaginary fists and legs to beat it from my father. I was inside its gaseous head, but I knew angels were creeping up to me from below, urged on by Seraphiel to drag me back to him. I forced my hand to my mouth, my lips over the last drops of Pandora's blood. I licked at them like a drowning girl desperate for dry land. Blood flowed down my throat and sank into every pore of my being. I pressed again with my brain, and the angel split asunder like smoke blown away by a hairdryer.

Then I caught Gabriel before he fell to the ground. Below me were hatred and confusion and a thousand angel wings beating in frustration. I heard Seraphiel before I saw him, a loud howl of despair as he flew at me with the spear aimed straight for my head. He was an inch from me when I teleported us both to the last place I'd felt safe.

We landed in the middle of a cemetery. Electric lights illuminated the graves, highlighting the path up to the church. Gabriel hung in my arms, as light as a feather, even though he was taller than me.

'Where are we, Cassie?'

I lifted him and propped him against a tombstone. The wind brought the chill of the night over us and he shivered inside his rags.

'We're in Whitby, near the Church of Saint Mary.' I scanned our surroundings, searching for danger, finding nothing but a rabbit hopping between the graves. Its eyes were pinpoints of red glaring in the gloom as it stared at me. Then, a noise above me made me jump. Peering up, I expected Seraphiel to dive towards me with that spear. But instead, I saw a group of birds hovering above my head. I thought it might be a murder of crows, but the sky was too dark to see them properly, even with the electric lights.

Gabriel slipped from the tombstone and slumped into the grass of the cemetery. I rushed to him; his eyes were drowsy and his breathing was fragile. And I didn't feel too good myself. The last of Pandora's blood had left my system. I knew it.

'You saved us, Cassandra.' Gabriel's grip was weak on my wrist.

'Call me Cassie.' My legs trembled and I sat next to him so we could catch our breath. Then I saw the rabbit again, but this time it had friends. Not only another three or four rabbits, but squirrels, mice, two foxes, and at least half a dozen cats. As far as welcoming committees went, they seemed reasonably harmless.

Then the glowing red eyes appeared behind them and moved towards us.

It was the last thing I saw before I collapsed.

9 ALICE: NIGHTCLUBBING

Amy was queuing for the club as I got to the entrance. She removed money from her pocket.

'I'll pay for these, Alice.' She pointed to a poster on the wall. 'There's a gig on tonight.'

I checked my jacket for the phone my mother had given me and the credit card from Angie. At least I'd be able to buy some drinks. A bunch of twenty-somethings got in the queue behind me. They all wore shirts emblazoned with the name of tonight's band: The Hex Pistols. I had no idea who they were, but I was curious to see them play.

The people started laughing and I glanced at the girl closest to me. She wore an utterly reflective top and it was distracting seeing me in her. I tried not to glance at my reflection, wondering if I'd always been this person inside of me, this girl ready to kill to get what she wanted. Perhaps not to kill, but maybe I'd always been prepared to hurt others to satisfy my needs. If that was so, was it time which had brought it out of me, or the Nephilim legacy inherited from my mother?

But what about the archangel blood flowing through

me, passed down from my father? Weren't angels supposed to be heavenly creatures of extraordinary grace and goodness? I guessed not since the one I'd met in Hollywood tried to suck my soul from me using a plastic straw, while the two archangels I'd encountered, Michael and Lucy, were dangerous and untrustworthy.

I continued to peer at my reflection in the girl's dress, wondering if all I was, was a product of my genetics and I had no free will of my own, no control over what I did beyond following the path of the Arcane.

It all came down to genetics again, just like I'd said back at the Foundation building about supernatural evolution. I stared at my hands while people were having fun around me, those a bit older than me doing what they should at that age: enjoying life with no worries of responsibility.

I twisted a little so I only saw a half of my face in the dress, looking as if I'd lost part of my ear. It made me wonder again where Cassie was, my mind drifting back to the last time I'd seen her on the grass in London just before Lucy separated us and we set off to save the world.

I dawdled for a second as the queue moved. It was only when Amy dragged me forward by the hand I returned to the present. She paid the entrance fee and we stumbled past the cloakroom.

There were two rooms to the club: a bar on our right and the venue for the music straight ahead. The place was already half full when we got in, and a support group of three women thumped electronic keyboards while warbling about the demise of the patriarchy. They finished their song and left the stage to a warm reception, and I was sorry we'd missed their set.

I headed for the bar before the rest of the crowd did.

'What do you want to drink, Amy?' I squeezed between

two burly blokes who smelt as if they hadn't bathed in a while. The DJ played something loud and it put a spring in my step even though I wasn't moving.

Amy pushed up to the back of my neck, her breath heavy on my skin. 'Get me a pint of cider.'

The guy behind the bar stared at me in expectation. 'I'll have fizzy water and a pint of cider, please.'

For one second, I thought he'd refuse to serve me since I was underage, but he only sneezed before getting the order. Sharp elbows poked me in the ribs as I waited, and I had to control my rising temper. I'd forgotten how much I hated being around groups of people. I paid for the drinks as the cider overflowed on to my hand and left it smelling of sweet apples. I slipped from the bar and gave Amy her drink. She seemed ecstatic as she took it from me.

'Where do you want to stand?'

I glanced across the venue, ignoring the customers with their hair reaching to the ceiling and the group of teenage girls all dressed in black. The sweat was already rising as a middle-aged bloke wearing an Elvis T-shirt slumped against the wall while people walked around him. The toilets were at the rear next to the sound engineer, and the floor was on two levels, with the one below sloping into the stage.

I headed for the seats.

'Let's sit down while we wait.' There was no point standing all night.

Amy looked through the crowd between drinking. 'I can't see anyone I know.'

I sipped at my drink to clear the sand growing at the back of my throat and stared at her.

'Have you been here before?'

She nodded. 'A few times. It's that far from the city centre, it doesn't attract the usual idiots, getting a mix of students, older music fans, and locals.' She licked at the booze on her top lip. 'I've been to a few gigs here.'

'Did you think Malika would be here?'

'I wasn't sure what to expect.'

A group of women screamed in Japanese from the speakers.

'She won't be here, Amy. We have to wait for the gang to approach me, and then go with them.'

Cider glistened on her mouth. 'Oh.'

'That's why I wanted you to stay away.' The water bubbled between my lips and down my throat.

She placed her free hand on mine. 'I can't leave you on your own, Alice.' Her words made me wonder if she'd received orders from my mother to stick with me all night.

We sat drinking while the DJ continued to play music. It was twenty minutes before the main band came on stage, and it was like I'd never fallen into the supernatural world and had been returned to the university bar where my journey had begun. Amy told me about her studies and how she'd joined the Foundation. I spoke about my brief time at uni and how, one day, I'd go back to finish my degree.

More people filled the venue, so there was little room to move when The Hex Pistols started their set. The band were four women looking not much older than me, bouncing up and down on stage with endless energy. We couldn't see a lot from where we were, so Amy dragged us from our seats towards the front of the stage. As the group got into position, Amy returned to the bar, and I leant over a speaker next to the lead singer's feet.

The music was loud, energetic and made me feel more alive than I had since my separation from Cassie. Most of the crowd were women and girls, and even though the band possessed angry energy, there was no feeling of danger or violence in the club. So I let myself go with the rhythm, dancing and bumping into those near me, watching Amy spill a drink on the floor while she flailed her arms around like a confused windmill.

I'm not sure how long it lasted, but the time seemed to flow by, a euphoric experience unlike anything I'd had before. In less than a month, I'd visited Hell, Limbo and Purgatory; beaten the Devil at cards to save my life; sailed across the sea on the *Flying Dutchman*; teleported, flown, and turned invisible; met and fought countless legendary creatures; discovered an identical twin sister I'd never known I had and found my mother. And I'd even saved the world.

But now, on this dance floor, swirling to the music with the crowd, I felt truly alive for the first time.

And the guilt came crashing through me because I was enjoying myself while Cassie was rotting inside a jail somewhere in America.

Energy seeped out of me as I pushed the guilt into the corner of my mind and remembered what I was there for: to save an abducted girl.

Disappointment surged through the crowd when the band finally left the stage after two encores. It was nearly ten-thirty and there'd been no sign of any drug gang. Amy was chatting to a green-haired woman as the lights came up and people sloped out of the club. I tapped on her shoulder.

'It looks like it's been a bust.'

She took a piece of paper from her new friend and grinned at me. 'Not for me, it hasn't.' There was a slight slurring to her words, which made me think she'd nipped to the bar without telling me; that or she couldn't hold her drink.

'Let's get out of here and head to the Foundation.'

I stepped over discarded plastic glasses and empty beer cans. A few people milled around to chat with the band. In an earlier time, a few months ago, I might have done the same, but the euphoria of the night had transformed into disappointment at not getting a lead to find Malika.

And all that guilt about Cassie festered away inside me.

Amy continued to grin as we headed from the club and towards the road. I turned to her, happy to get a taxi to the Foundation since my legs throbbed from the dancing. She was talking to a group of women. When I approached her, I realised one of them had a knife pushed up to her stomach.

The tallest strode to me. 'She tells us you're the witch; is that right?'

I forced my voice to tremble as I replied. 'Don't hurt us; please, don't hurt us.'

They glanced at each other as if they'd won the lottery. The tall one grabbed me and dragged me towards a waiting car. The others tossed Amy and me into the back. The tall one joined us, knife in hand, while the other two got into the front seats. The car pulled off with nobody speaking.

I squeezed Amy's leg; this is what I'd wanted. It didn't matter if they had knives because I was confident I could handle them. We drove in the dark for twenty minutes, away from the city and into the outskirts. When the car stopped, we were bundled out and into a run-down housing estate. The relics of burnt-out cars lined the roads as feral cats scrambled over them; the entire place stank of crap and desperation.

The tall woman pushed me towards the closest dilapidated house. The windows were boarded over and the front door looked like it had been kicked in more than once. The three of them laughed as we entered the dump.

'Turn right into the living room,' the tall one said.

We did as she commanded, only to call it a living room was a lie of the highest order. The place stank of vomit, with rotten food cartons everywhere. I doubted anyone had ever lived in there; this was barely an existence.

Two sizeable lumps slithered from the shadows and leaned forward. The larger of them spoke through broken glass. 'Well done, Jacky; that's an excellent job.'

I peered at the woman who'd spoken. 'What do you want with us?'

'We don't care about her.' She pointed at Amy as someone threw my new friend to the floor. 'We might sell her to the traffickers, but it's you we desire.' She stepped towards me and I wished I was back in the Foundation building, which smelt of nothing. Instead, an aroma surrounded her that would make Death weep.

'What do you want me for?' I glanced over my shoulder. The tall woman was behind me, her two friends blocking the door. They all seemed unsteady on their feet. I assumed they must have been sampling some of their product. This would be easier than I thought; once I found Malika.

The lump nodded to her underling. 'Bring the other one out, Jacky.'

Jacky stepped out of the room and into somewhere else. After two minutes, she came back with Malika, who was gagged and had her hands bound.

'Why would you abduct her and us?' I was using the time to decide which one to take down first. If I could deal with the leader quickly, the others might give up and run.

The lump's grin revealed a mouth only half full of teeth. And most of them hadn't seen a toothbrush in a while.

'Don't pretend with me, kid.' She pointed a bony finger at Malika. 'We know what she's capable of. If you can do the same, then the two of you will make us very rich once we get you out of this country.'

'And what if I can't do what she does?'

The tall one was close to me with the knife in her hand. It would be easy to take it from her and get the three of us out. But I waited, though the smell was clawing at the sides of my gut. I'd need another shower after being there, and some fresh clothes.

The lump strode closer to me. 'Then we'll spend tonight feeding on your soul.'

A chill shot around the room as she started to shake and change, her flesh wobbling inside her clothes like jelly in a bowl. I reached down and pulled Amy up and moved towards the far side. The rest of the drug gang joined their sister in a twisted shape-shifting transformation, resembling a musical girl group on acid.

Amy trembled in my arm. 'What's... what's happening?'

I pushed my back into the damp concrete and stared at them, transfixed: their heads grew wider, arms longer and thicker, with their legs tall enough to drive them close to the ceiling four feet above us.

'I don't know, Amy.'

The only thing I knew was, whatever it was, it wouldn't be good for us.

10 CASSIE: WHITBY

The red eyes had gone when I awoke in a soft bed in a room full of fresh flowers smelling of strawberries. My arms and legs ached as I pulled the covers back and wondered why that fruity aroma was getting closer to me. I fell out of the bed when the ogre leaned over and said my name.

'Cassie Arcane.'

I hit the floor with a thump. My elbow banged into the carpet and my hip bumped into a table. The ogre peered at me through pea-green eyes, its head out of proportion with the body. Where it wasn't covered with hair, it had bright orange skin.

'Who are you?' It was all I could think to say as I pushed myself back into the wall.

'I am Polyphemus and you are Cassie Arcane.'

The shock left me, replaced by irritation that someone, some ogre, was in my bedroom without permission. At least I was still dressed, and this wasn't my bedroom. I flexed my muscles, stood, and addressed the intruder.

'Where is Vika Vistala?'

'That is why I'm here, Cassie Arcane. Vika Vistala requests your presence in the dining room, where dinner is served.'

My elbow throbbed, so I rubbed it. 'Dinner? What time is it?'

'It's eight o'clock, Cassie Arcane. You've slept for nearly twenty-two hours.'

And it felt like it. 'Okay, but I have to wash my face and brush my teeth before anything else.' It was as if I'd woken from some terrible nightmare. But then I remembered the warring angels and Gabriel. 'What happened to my companion?'

'All will be revealed in time. Everything you need is in the bathroom, Cassie Arcane. I'll wait here for you.'

I puffed out my cheeks and walked around him. He was right about the bathroom, and there was even a fresh set of clothes for me. I left them there and stared into the mirror. At first, I didn't see myself but Alice, until I touched my damaged ear and remembered who I was. I threw water over my face. There were still aches and pains everywhere, but now I felt as if I was close to my sister. I'd survived the American prison, defeated Pandora, and rescued my father from the angels in the Devastation; it wouldn't be long before I found Alice, and we'd kill Dracula and get our mother back.

That thought shocked me and I pulled away from the mirror. Why did I think about killing the vampire? With my Arcane abilities, I should be able to get my mother away from him without resorting to murder.

Then there was Gabriel, our father. I turned off the hot water and imagined the impossible happening: Alice and I reunited with our parents. It was all I thought about as I brushed my teeth and cleaned the rest of the dirt from my hands, remembering how Pandora's dried blood had sparked my Arcane abilities to escape Seraphiel and his horde.

The ogre stood opposite me when I exited the bathroom.

'Where is the person who was with me, Polyphemus?'

'Vika Vistala will reveal all.'

With that, he turned and left, so I followed. It was a long corridor where the carpet was on the walls, ceiling, and floor. That's when I noticed he didn't have any shoes or socks, and his huge toes wriggled in the comfort as we walked.

It was tempting to follow suit and throw off my footwear, but all I focused on was how good it was to be back inside the Impossible Palace. At least I wasn't following the path I'd taken the first time I came here when everything was gravity-defying staircases and foul human-headed spiders waiting to devour you if you fell from those peculiar steps.

We walked for two minutes before entering a vast dining hall. There was no carpet there, only a dark wood flooring, walls adorned with glittering swords, shields and emblems, and a giant table taking up most of the room. Food covered it, with many sweet aromas drifting through the air: cooked meat, roasted vegetables, rice and pasta, slices of bread of all types and flavours, plus fruits, cakes and other sugary stuff.

At the head stood the Guardian of the Impossible Palace: Vika Vistala.

'I prepared a feast fit for a conquering hero.' She held her hands out and smiled at me.

Part of me wanted to throw my arms around her because I was back on friendly turf, but I hardly knew her.

She'd allowed Scooby, her Hellhound, to take Alice and me to Hell to find our mother, but it wasn't out of the goodness of her heart. In return, she'd received the guardianship of this place from our friend, Kai the Warwitch. So, I smiled and went to her.

'You've done a grand job with this spread, Vika, but as hungry as I am, I don't think I'll eat all this.'

She came forward and slapped me on the arm. 'It's not all for you, silly. Some guests will join us once you update me on everything that's happened since I saw you in Edinburgh.' Vika had cut her long hair into a short fringe, its colour matching the green of her lipstick. She brushed some fluff from her suit and presented her widest smile.

'Speaking of guests, where's the man I was with in the cemetery?'

She scratched her chin and looked confused. 'Were you in a cemetery? I found you face down outside a pub.'

'What?'

Vika slapped me on the arm again. 'Don't worry; I'm lying, just as you are.'

I stepped back from her. 'I don't know what you're talking about.'

'Best you follow me, then.' She turned on her heels and went through the door behind her. She waited for me, so I followed, striding into a small space like a broom cupboard. Before I could say anything, she switched off the light and darkness engulfed us.

'Stop playing games, Vika.' An irritating cricket beat its legs against the back of my skull. Then illumination returned and we were somewhere else: Gabriel was on a bed with tubes in his arms. I rushed to him.

'Is he okay?' I grabbed his hand. His skin was cold, his eyes unmoving, but his chest was; only slowly.

'The angel is in a deep sleep, what the humans call a coma.' She sat in a chair in the corner and filed her nails. 'What did the two of you get up to?'

I flopped into a seat and told her everything, from leaving her place in Edinburgh to escaping the Devastation. She listened to every moment with a fascinated gaze, her eyes narrowing and widening at different times, with an occasionally opened mouth. She looked as tired as I felt at the end.

'So that's it all.' I watched Gabriel during my account. 'Do you know what's wrong with him?'

'He's lost his wings and his Grace; in that form, he's only human now. I suppose the suffering he endured in that cell, then the exhaustion of you rescuing him and the effort to teleport here must have all taken their toll.'

'Can you help him?' Pain seeped through me again.

She got up. 'Let's eat. The guests should be there now, and perhaps one of them can waken your father.'

We left the room and went into a smaller one, similar to the broom cupboard we'd used to get there. I put my fingers on the blank wall.

'What is this, Vika?'

'It's a transportation device.' Her hand was on the light switch. 'Like your teleportation ability, but it only works within the Impossible Palace. But the Palace is a big place. I've only explored a quarter of it since taking over the guardianship.'

'Why do you turn the light off?'

She laughed. 'If you saw what we travel through to get from one point to another, you'd probably lose your mind.'

Then she switched the light off and I suddenly felt nervous in the dark. When she turned it on, we were in the dining room again; and it was packed. Sitting at every seat was, from first appearance, a collection of supernatural creatures helping themselves to the food and drink. There must have been over two dozen there.

Polyphemus was the largest of them, but I also recognised a leprechaun, goblin, sprite, faun, and werewolf. The others were all unknown to me, but each of them watched me as they ate.

'What is this, Vika?' I kept my focus on the werewolf, clenching my fists and waiting for it to attack.

Vika put her hand on my arm. 'Relax, Cassie; no one is here to harm you.' She let go and pointed at the table. 'Everyone here is a refugee.'

'Refugees from what?'

'The world is a changed place after what you and your sister did to those two leaders of humanity. Governments, politicians, influential individuals and groups are now taking a lot more interest in the supernatural.' Rufus, the cat, came and brushed against Vika's leg. 'Supernatural beings are disappearing from British towns and cities, snatched from the street and never seen again.' She picked up the moggy. 'At first, I thought there might have been an increase in assassins after the events with the president and the prime minister.'

'Assassins?'

'Yes, like you, Cassie. Isn't that what you did before you met your sister?' I didn't reply. 'The supernatural world has tried to hide from whoever is doing this. So I opened the Impossible Palace to those scared for their lives. All are welcome here, and it is a vast place.' She leant into me. 'Feeding them and stopping the squabbles are the hardest parts.'

Here before me was another consequence of my actions, and she was right. I had spent two years killing the things I called monsters before bumping into Alice in that park.

'And you don't know who is doing it?'

She shook her head. 'My contacts across the country say the same thing: it's an organised group, but we haven't discovered who yet.'

'Have you searched the streets of Whitby to catch them in the act?'

Her shoulders slumped and she dropped Rufus to the floor. I was aware of every eye in the room scrutinising us.

'I haven't left this place since I took over from Kai.' Darkness consumed her face.

'Why not, Vika?'

'In the last month, in Whitby alone, twelve vampires of my acquaintance have gone missing or been murdered. Moreover, there are rumours of experiments carried out on those abducted.' She peered at me. 'Experiments conducted on them while they're awake.'

She tried to hide it by keeping her arm pinned to her side and away from the others, but she struggled to keep it from shaking. The great Scottish vampire, the Baobhan Sith was afraid; the woman who inspired fear into the Edin-burgh underworld was incapable of leaving this place because she was scared.

'I'll help you discover who is doing this, Vika. But I need to get my father out of his coma and find Alice and my mother.' I put my hand in hers, helping her to steady the shaking.

'I might be able to aid you with all of that.' She let go of me and turned to the table. 'Is Toriyama here?'

The chatter in the room decreased and a supernatural peeled away from the others; a small monkey with a human-like face strode towards us. Rufus snarled and ran into the corner.

The monkey spoke. 'How can I help?' Vika bent, held out her hand, and the talking monkey took it. They stayed like that for a few seconds before letting go. The monkey nodded. 'I'll try.' Then it returned to the feast.

Vika turned to me. 'Toriyama is a Satori and can read minds. Once he's eaten and rested, he'll try with Gabriel and see what's keeping him in that coma.'

'Great.' I grabbed Vika's hand and led her to the table. 'Once I've refuelled, you and I are going into Whitby to find out who is abducting and killing supernaturals.'

11 ALICE: MALIKA

A cacophony of shrieks echoed around the room. Four trolls loomed over us, two at the door, the leader and her deputy ahead. They all carried knives with them, but I doubted they'd need them, considering the vicious-looking claws extending from their fingers and cutting into the carpet. They licked their lips and slavered over the rug.

I stared at the one who'd spoken to me before. 'You can let us leave and go back to your secret world.'

The creature let out a terrible laugh, which made my ears burn. Then she reached behind her and picked up what I thought was a chicken leg. Only when I smelt the blood on it did I recognise it as human. The troll took a bite before throwing the rest to the two guarding the door.

'You and the other witch are coming with us.' Then she pointed a claw at Amy. 'But it's a long journey from here to the boat, so we'll snack on her first.'

My heart thumped against my ribs as I glanced at Malika on the floor, her body pushed against a tatty sofa. There was a coffee table between the leader and us, but that exposed us to the two guarding the door. Amy grabbed hold of my arm, her fingers trembling at the same frequency as her voice.

'We can't get out, Alice.'

The trolls did nothing but grunt and growl in our direction. I wondered how many times they'd done this before, recognising the arrogance in their twisted faces. Amy pushed closer to me, her cheek knocking my jacket open enough for me to see the dried blood of the Morningstar clinging to the leather. I could lick that up and this would be over in a second.

'Just like a drug,' I whispered.

Amy shivered next to me. 'What?'

I ignored her and focused on those beasts waiting to pounce. I wouldn't use Lucy's blood; Mother had said she was stronger and faster than most other creatures because of her Nephilim DNA. And I had that, and genes from my archangel father. I might be a few years away from reaching my full potential, but I was still the Arcane. I didn't need any extra help to deal with trolls.

I pushed Amy to the floor and reached for the coffee table; it was just the right size to pick up in one hand. My fingers dug into the wood and I swung it behind me, enjoying the strength in my arm as I flexed my muscles. I brought the table around, the force of it thrusting the edge into the guts of the closest troll. Blood sprayed across the door and walls as it split in half. Everything appeared to happen in slow motion as the top of the troll fell towards Amy. She stood there open-mouthed as the troll's legs tumbled in Malika's direction, running at her like a headless chicken.

The dying beast let out a great howl that rattled the windows. The other three appeared frozen in shock. This wasn't supposed to happen to them in their lair. I used their confusion to my advantage, swooping down to scoop up the discarded knife. Then I jumped as high as I could, surprising myself by lifting well off the ground. It was enough to bring me up to the neck of the remaining troll at the door. I flashed the blade across its flesh. I landed on the floor at the same time as its decapitated head. It would only be a matter of seconds before the others attacked me.

I lifted Amy. 'Take Malika and get out of here.'

Before she could reply, I had the coffee table in one hand and the knife in the other. I sprang at the remaining trolls, smashing the front of the table into them, so we went sprawling into the wall. As I bounced off the stone, I saw Amy drag Malika outside.

The beasts and I rose together. I pushed the furniture into the troll leader while slashing at her chest, a frenzied stabbing that made my hand ache. A long, narrow fist caught me on the cheek and I slumped backwards. Pain consumed me as she lunged towards me, dripping blood everywhere as those great claws grasped for my eyes. They missed by inches as she fell past me.

Blood and guts spiralled out of the leader as her deputy cowered in the corner. Her body shimmered and shook, the transformation taking only ten seconds as she returned to her former self. She pushed her legs away from her dying leader and stared at me.

'You've done me a favour, kid. I never liked any of this lot.'

I kept my eye on her as the other one groaned in death. 'That doesn't mean I won't kill you.' The bloodied knife was in front of me as I stepped towards her. She cowered against the wall.

'Please, I promise this won't happen again.' She glanced at the twitching mess close to her. 'It was all her doing.'

I knelt and wiped the blade on the dying troll's leg. 'And why should I trust you?'

'Malika told us about the Foundation and the work they're doing in the city for people like us.' Thinking she was like me made my stomach turn.

'You want to help the Foundation?'

She buried her face in her hands and sobbed, her voice muffled through damp fingers. 'Anything is better than this.' Her eyes were tired as she lifted her head. 'My parents were human; they couldn't wait to get rid of me once they found out what a monster I was. Eventually, after living on the streets, I was taken in by the other trolls. It was the only way I could survive.'

Did I believe any of this? It would have been easy to lean across and slit her throat. I looked around the room, the stink of blood, guts and death filling every inch. I was sick of killing.

'Are there any more hostages here?' She shook her head. 'Do you know where the Foundation building is?'

She nodded. 'I do.'

'Show up tomorrow and ask for Alice. Can you do that?'

'I will.'

'Good.' I scanned the carnage I'd caused. 'What will you do about this?'

She wiped the tears from her face. 'Don't worry; there are little ones who need feeding.'

With that terrible thought in my mind, I turned from her and left the house. And then something dreadful gripped my heart: Amy and Malika weren't in the street.

'Shit!' I twisted every which way to search across the estate, but it was empty apart from stray dogs and abandoned cars. I removed the phone from my pocket and called Amy's number. The shrill ringing of the device was only a few feet from me, coming from near the burnt-out vehicles.

Perhaps they'd hidden behind them.

I ran to them while dogs howled at the moon. At least I hoped they were dogs. This entire estate might be a haven for the supernatural; werewolves, vampires, and ghouls could attack me at any moment.

My legs skipped over empty pizza boxes and crushed glass as I reached the cars. The sound of the phone came from the ground. Were they underneath a metal husk? I forgot about the danger and crouched, the cold concrete of the pavement nipping at my hand as I placed my palm down.

The mobile continued to sing as I located it, abandoned below the car in the middle of the road. My knees creaked as I bent to get it. I stopped the call and slipped both devices into my jacket.

The night clung to me like an oppressive blanket. I had no choice but to shout their names, regardless of whatever creatures my voice would bring to the party. I was sucking in air, ready to yell when someone tapped me on the shoulder. I spun around and grabbed Amy by the throat.

I let go immediately. 'Sorry.' My cheeks flushed and heat swam through me. Malika stood next to her, and behind them was a taxi with its engine running. The excitement of the trolls must have affected my senses.

Amy placed a hand on her neck and coughed. 'I've got us a lift out of here.' She nodded at the vehicle. 'What happened in the house? Are you okay?'

'I'm fine.' I grabbed her arm and pulled her towards the car. There was an old man in the driver's seat, bald on top but with a huge grey beard covering the rest of his face.

'Who is this?' He appeared harmless, but appearances could be deceptive in this world.

Malika spoke for the first time. 'This is Ali; he went to school with my dad.'

That was good enough for me. I climbed into the front passenger seat and let them get into the back. I didn't care how they'd found this guy as long as we returned to the Foundation quickly.

Amy leant forward and dropped a tenner into his hand. 'Do you know where the Foundation building is, Ali?'

He nodded and was off before any of us could say anything else. I left Amy and Malika whispering to each other and kept my eyes on the road ahead. My fingers ached and I stared at my palm. There were more lines there than before, just like with my face. I was tired, but I felt great. I'd dealt with those trolls without having to use archangel blood. I'd made my mind up never to drink that stuff again. I'd rely on myself from now; no more supping from the flesh of angels or demons.

The neon lights of shops, bars and restaurants whizzed by in a glow, illuminating the gloom and bringing darkness into the light. That's what my mother and Dr Silk were doing with the Foundation: bringing darkness into the light, and I was determined to help them as much as possible while waiting for news about Cassie. The longer I was here, the stronger I'd get, and the stronger I was, the more use I'd be to my sister when I got to America.

I stared out of the window and remembered the troll I'd left behind in that house. Had I done the right thing? Drug dealers were bad, but those creatures were worse. By leaving one of them alive, had I condemned others to death and imprisonment? The more I thought about it, the more I questioned what I'd done. Killing the trolls had been easy, not just in action, but in how simple it had been in my mind. Was it all part of my heritage?

Numerous terrible thoughts crowded inside my head and, before I knew it, we were at the Foundation. We slipped out of the car, Malika giving Ali a warm embrace before he drove away. The greenery shimmered around the lights of the building.

I was striding up the steps until a hand stopped me. It was Malika.

'I never thanked you for what you did: you saved me.'

Something deep inside her lit up her eyes, a palpable joy spreading across the whole of her face. She took my hands and brought them to her cheeks. Her skin was warm, an aroma of blossoms drifting from her hair. She let go and smiled.

'Is it true what they said about you, that you're a witch who can transform substances into different things?'

She laughed and skipped up the steps. 'I'm sure we'll get to know each other very well over the coming weeks, Alice Arcane.'

Then she disappeared through the door, and Amy and I followed her. Dr Silk and my mother waited for us inside. Malika threw her arms around the doctor, but only gave my mother a curious look. I'd forgotten she was new here and still a stranger to most people. In reality, she was still a stranger to me. But I'd change that.

'Well done, you two,' she said before taking my hand. 'You've made me a very proud mother, Alice.' She seemed pleased for me, but there was also apprehension etched below her eyes. She pulled me away from the others.

'What's wrong, Mother?'

She let go of me and took a deep breath. 'We've had some news about Cassie.'

My heart leapt, thumping against my ribs as if ready to break out of prison. 'You've found where she is?'

Her face darkened and she shook her head. 'Not quite.' She glanced over to where Dr Silk was speaking to the girls. 'Julius has contacts in the US, and they've heard rumours coming from the FBI.'

'The FBI? Did they lock Cassie away?'

'At first, yes, that's what we were told. After your sister killed the president and slaughtered his cabinet, some wanted her sent to trial or even put to death, but other prominent voices desired something else for Cassie.' The pain in her voice was unmistakable.

'What did they want her for?'

'There's a new world order now regarding how the human authorities deal with the supernatural.'

'I know: some people want to kill us, while others want to work with us.'

She shook her head. 'I'm afraid it's worse than that, Alice. They don't want to work with supernatural creatures; they want to use them for their own ends, regardless of how terrible they are.'

What she said made me laugh. 'Cassie would never work with anyone in authority; she told me so herself.'

Mother placed a hand on my shoulder. 'That's not what we've heard, Alice.' She let out a long sigh. 'It seems as if your sister is working with the US government; they've turned her into their super-soldier.'

12 CASSIE: VIKA

I ate in relative silence while the rest chatted around me. Vika played the perfect host, but she couldn't hide her nervousness from me; had the deaths and abductions affected her this much? I found it hard to believe, but she'd reluctantly agreed to join me in the streets of Whitby once we'd eaten. I hoped it would take my mind off Gabriel's coma and where Alice and my mother were.

Vika wasn't the only one with a nervous twitch. A young blonde woman sitting next to me couldn't keep her fingers still as she played with the food and sipped at her drink. I finished mine and was pushing the plate away when she spoke.

'I shouldn't be here.' She nibbled at fingernails bitten to the point of non-existence. 'I'm not like the rest of you.'

'What do you mean?'

She pulled a hand from her mouth and offered it to me. 'Hi, I'm Susan Saxon.'

I shook it, noticing how cold she was even though it was warm in the room. 'I'm Cassie.'

Her smile was wide and engaging. 'Everyone here knows who you are; you saved the world.'

I blushed a little. 'Well, I don't know about that, plus I had some help.' The deep blue of her eyes distracted me. 'Why shouldn't you be here?'

'Because I'm not like them. I'm...' For one second, I thought she was about to say normal. 'I'm human.'

'Why should that be a problem?'

She glanced over at Vika. 'Oh, it isn't, but I feel like I'm taking someone else's place, that's all.'

'I'm sure Vika had a good reason for inviting you in. Do you want to talk about it?' I was eager to get outside and stretch my legs as a free person for the first time in an eternity, but it was apparent she needed to unburden herself.

'I ran away from a cult.' She said it in such a matter-of-fact manner, I thought she was joking at first; until I recognised the pain in her eyes.

'You don't need to talk about it.' Susan took hold of my hand and it seemed like a big decision for her to do that. I placed my other hand on top of hers. 'But I'm here to listen.'

Her lips narrowed as her eyelids blinked rapidly. 'My parents took me there when I was fourteen; that was twelve years ago. The Church of the Eternal Light, they call it, but it's not a church at all; not for anything good anyway.' She took a deep breath and glanced around the room, watching the others eat, drink, and talk away. I wondered if she was as lonely in the outside world as she appeared here.

'You're safe in here, Susan.' I stared at the array of supernatural creatures with us, surprised at how at ease she was near them, and then I guessed she'd seen a lot worse in her life.

Time ticked by and I had to leave; I removed my hands from hers and stood. 'We'll talk some more when I return.'

Susan smiled again and got up. 'I'd like that, Cassie.' She reached into her trouser pocket. 'Will you tell my husband I'm okay?' She handed me a piece of paper with a name and address on it. 'I haven't seen him for weeks and he'll be worried sick.'

'Of course, I will.' She seemed happy as she left and I felt good at doing something for her. Saving the world and defeating evil was fine, but the small things made everything worthwhile.

'Toriyama has gone to see your father.' Vika was at my side. 'Are you sure you want to head into town?' She couldn't hide the reluctance in her voice.

I showed her the paper.

'Absolutely. We've got somewhere to go now.'

The last time I'd visited the Impossible Palace, I'd exited through a fridge. Now it was more conventional, stepping through a massive wooden door and into the cemetery where I'd collapsed after teleporting from the Devastation. When I turned around, the exit was gone, replaced by graves and tombstones. It was night again, the air filled with moths darting for the moon. The smell of seawater seeped in over the cliffs, with the mist settling in my hair. Vika had changed into a dark black outfit of a tight jacket and even tighter jeans. When she moved out of the moonlight, it was hard to see her.

'We need to go towards the whalebone arch. That's near where this John Saxon lives.' She pointed over my head and we set off to find Susan's husband.

I went down the steps from the Abbey, looking out over the town and remembering when I'd taken the same path with Alice the first time. We'd been going in the opposite direction then, struggling up on a sweltering day in our search for Kai, the Warwitch. A cool breeze swept across my face as I considered where my sister and Kai were now and thought about how much had changed in such a short space of time.

As we entered the street at the bottom, a group on a guided tour approached us, listening intently to a tale of the town's history. We dodged them as Vika strode next to me. I thought it would be a silent journey towards the Saxon house, with me struggling for a way to approach the subject of Vika's fears, but once we stepped on to the bridge across the river, she opened up.

'Drinking angel blood, or the blood of something born from the Heavenly Host, can't be good for you.'

We headed to North Terrace, striding past pubs and takeaways, the aroma of alcohol mixing with fresh pizza and cooked meat. My stomach churned a little, but it wasn't from hunger after what I'd eaten; the taste of Pandora's blood lingered in the back of my head.

'I don't intend to do it again.' I thought about the occasions I had. 'I didn't know what was happening with Lucy the first time because she lied to us and tricked me. With Pandora, it was purely accidental during the fight with her; and with the angels in the Devastation, it was a necessity. So I don't feel bad for any of those events.' This wasn't true because two constant pains nagged at me: one was in the pit of my stomach like a terrible case of food poisoning; the other lurked in the corner of my mind and scratched at my flesh.

We strode up a street on the opposite side to a huge queue outside a fish shop, the aroma of salt and vinegar hanging in the air.

'How do you know Gabriel is your father? It could all be another ruse from Lucy or Michael.'

I had no doubts about it. 'Blood will find blood. Plus, I recognised myself in his eyes; I saw Alice there.'

'You must miss your sister.' There was a deep sadness in her voice and I realised I knew nothing about her, apart from what we'd learned in Edinburgh.

'I'll find Alice and my mother once this is over and Gabriel wakens. Then we'll be reunited as a family.' I wondered what it would be like; if we'd be happy or just a bunch of strangers brought together into a bizarre world. And what did Gabriel want to tell me about my mother?

Several amusement arcades were ahead of us and I decided this would be the best time to speak about Vika's fears. There was a bench on my right, so I sat on it.

'Did you do that on purpose?' Vika said. I thought she meant me talking about her worries, until she pointed to the plaque behind me and I read what was on it.

'This is the spot where Bram Stoker was inspired to write Dracula.' I appreciated the irony. From this position, there would have been a direct view to the Abbey and the cemetery we'd just left, if someone hadn't erected a wooden fence between the path and the cliff.

Vika sat next to me. 'It is, but what they don't mention is Dracula met Stoker here and told the writer some of his life story. They had a conversation, as we are now.'

It seemed the perfect time to broach a complex subject. 'What happened after Alice and I left Edinburgh, Vika? Where did Kai go?' I missed my friend, the Warwitch.

She pushed a stray purple hair from her face. 'Kai stayed in Edinburgh and is still there, as far as I know. I came straight here and started the work you witnessed tonight with the refugees.' The wind swept across both of us. 'The world is a much more dangerous place now, Cassie, even for the likes of me.' Vika lifted her jacket and shirt to show me the mark on her hip: a jagged wound from something which had cut deep into her.

'What did that to you?'

She ran a finger over the scar, and then touched it to her lips. 'I was born twice; once as a human, then as a vampire. These events were thirty years apart in the middle of Queen Victoria's reign. As a human, I had to fight to survive, through poverty, against a violent father and surrounded by men who wanted to hurt me. They all suffered when this happened to me.' She opened her mouth and bared her fangs. 'But by then, it was too late for my mother and daughter.' Vika paused and looked across the sea. 'Then, as a vampire, I was alone and in a strange place, struggling to endure against humans and others like me.'

'Vampires attacked you?'

Vika covered her scar. 'The vampire world mirrors the human one regarding male dominance and female subservience.' She laughed at my shocked face. 'What? Did you think all the monsters stick together like a big happy family?'

'You're not a monster, Vika.' Would it be too painful to ask her about her daughter?

She got up. 'It doesn't matter now.' She touched the scar through her clothes. 'I lied earlier when I said I hadn't left the Impossible Palace since coming to Whitby. When the refugee numbers increased, I went looking for the culprits one night, and they attacked me.' Vika's eyes peered right into me. 'I've had many fights in my time, Cassie, and I've suffered beatings like most, but this was different. They cut me with something I've never encountered before; hurt me with a weapon I can't heal from, and that's impossible.'

The chill in her voice penetrated my heart. 'What happened, Vika?'

'I'd gone out to scout the spot of the latest vampire disappearances.' She gazed beyond me. 'It wasn't far from here, and the night was much like this one. I was heading towards the skate park when two hooded figures approached me.'

'Weren't you worried?'

Vika laughed. 'I'm a hundred-and-fifty-year-old vampire, Cassie; what could worry me?' She tried to hide the tremble in her little finger, but I saw it.

'Did they attack you?'

'Not at first. I believed they were teenagers coming from the skate park, so thought nothing of it.' She glanced into the sky. 'I guess I was arrogant then, having come to a small seaside town from Edinburgh and what I'd done there.'

'You mean with the organised crime gangs?'

Vika nodded. 'Yes. You can never get rid of crime and its adherents entirely, but I'd curtailed the activities of most of the criminal gangs in Edinburgh before coming here, so I believed things would be a lot easier, even with the mysterious disappearances of several vampires. That overconfidence nearly got me killed.'

I pictured what might have happened to her that night.

'The two hooded figures walked past you, and then attacked?'

'They did. One of them stabbed me in the hip and I thought nothing of it.' Her hand went to the wound. 'Until the bleeding wouldn't stop and agony like molten lava shot through me.' She took her fingers away and peered at them. 'The only thing that saved me was a group of humans appeared and the attackers fled. I managed to get back to the Impossible Palace and one of our healers stopped the bleeding.'

'How long ago was this?'

Vika clenched her hand into a fist. 'It seems like it was only yesterday, but it was four weeks ago.'

I stood from the bench. 'We'll find who's doing this, Vika, I promise you that. And we'll make them pay.'

She smiled at me. 'I believe you, Cassandra Arcane. You've stopped the end of the world and escaped from an angel war. I don't think anything is beyond you.'

I resisted the urge to tell her not to put too much faith in me as we set off for the whalebone arch. We'd hardly gone ten feet when a dense mist stole in from the sea and obscured everything near us.

Vika was right next to me. 'Well, this is ominous.'

She wasn't wrong. We walked at a snail's pace towards the whalebone arch and the statue of Captain Cook near it, two explorers of the supernatural in a human world. The fog crept around us, reminding me of the blue mist which was an extension of Pandora. That nagging itch at the back of my head grew worse.

Finally, I saw the whalebone arch a few feet away and Vika stopped in front of me.

'What's wrong?' Silence surrounded us.

'Something is watching us from the top of the bones.'

Then the fog enclosed me and I couldn't see Vika anymore.

13 ALICE: EVOLUTION

I got little sleep that night. My mother's words scrambled around inside my brain, all mixed up in the wrong order and making no sense every time I revisited them. I switched on my phone and texted Medusa to take my mind off it. I poured out all my fears to her.

She replied immediately.

You can't trust anything until you get more information. And you have to speak to your sister.

I know, but it's driving me crazy.

You've had a hard day and a difficult time since Cassie left. You need a good night's sleep.

Then she sent me a photo of a dog wearing big glasses as it read *Animal Farm*.

LMAO! How are you?

Great. Sasha and I are getting on like a barn on fire.

Sasha was Medusa's blind online girlfriend.

When I've got everything sorted here, I must get Sasha over to meet you.

Don't worry about that. Find Cassie first.

And that was the last thing I read as I tried to sleep.

Initially, it came in fits and starts, my mind drifting into a tortured dreamland of Cassie dressed as a US soldier, toting an automatic rifle in each hand and spraying bullets everywhere. The violence of that shocked me awake, so I gave up and switched on the TV. The news stations were filled with nothing but disinformation, so I settled on a movie channel, flopping in front of some Leonardo DiCaprio flick where he's a cop on an island, searching for a missing woman. I must have dropped off eventually because I missed the end.

The TV was still flickering when I woke, the digital clock in the corner telling me it was nearly mid-day. I couldn't remember the last time I'd got up so late. My head throbbed, and my bones ached. I slipped out of bed to find a note stuffed under the door. I left it there and went into the bathroom. I needed to wash my face and brush my teeth before doing anything else.

I still smelt the dried blood on my jacket as I grabbed the paper from the floor. I wiped the last of the sleep from my eyes and read it. It was from my mother.

Enjoy a lie-in, and when you're ready, meet us in the basement. Use this key card for the lift.

There was an electronic card attached to the bottom of the note. I threw it on the bed and watched a cartoon cat chase a cartoon mouse on the TV as I dressed. I took my phone, saw no new messages, and put it into my trouser pocket. I thought of Cassie working for the American government and wondered if it had happened at the same time I was enjoying myself on the dance floor of that club.

And then I remembered killing those trolls and how good it had felt. Could I really blame Cassie if that's what she was doing: helping the Americans kill monsters? That's what she'd been doing when we'd first met, only now, if it was true, she was doing the same thing in another country. She was still saving lives, just like I'd done last night.

I shook the thoughts from my head and went downstairs. When I walked into the corridor, it seemed as if the previously smell-free building now had an aroma of something unknown about it.

Amy greeted me as I stepped from the lift.

'The kraken awakes.' She was back in her corporate white uniform with a huge grin on her face. Last night's danger didn't appear to have affected her. She was the only person in the room.

I walked across to the table and poured myself a glass of orange juice; lined up against the wall were bowls of fresh fruit and an array of sandwiches. I seized the shiniest apple and turned to her.

'Where's everyone else?'

'Mary and Dr Silk are in the annexe next door. They had a troll visitor this morning.'

I bit into an apple and chewed it loudly. 'Was it the one from last night?'

'Yes, the woman you left there; her name is Grace. She's going to join the Foundation as an outreach worker.'

I had done the right thing by leaving her alive. So perhaps I shouldn't doubt myself so much.

I pulled up a seat and grabbed a cheese sandwich at the same time. 'What does an outreach worker do?'

Amy sat opposite me. 'Well, before I knew the truth about the Foundation, the normal outreach workers would go into the community to help the city's most vulnerable: get the homeless into shelters, find employment or training courses for the unemployed; that sort of thing. But now, with our supernatural wing, I expect Grace will work with people like her.'

I finished the apple and dropped the core on to the table. 'Trolls?'

Amy shrugged. 'It's all new to me, but probably, and with other supernatural beings.'

'We should just call them Abbeys.'

'Abbeys?' Confusion filled her face.

'Short for abnormal, since we're the opposite of normal.'

'Is that how you feel about yourself?' Concern seeped from her eyes.

I bit into the sandwich. 'I've always felt that way, even before I found out I was the child of a Nephilim.'

'Why?' Amy said.

I swallowed the cheese and felt it drop into the hollow inside me.

'I spent sixteen years believing my parents had abandoned me. So I was passed from pillar to post between care facilities and foster homes, hardly able to find a connection with anyone, adult or kid. The one time I did, that person died of cancer just as I was getting to know her. Even when others surrounded me, I felt nothing but unending loneliness. It seemed that everyone had someone but me, and I guessed it was because I was nothing special in this big wide world.'

'But you are special, Alice, and never forget that.' My mother's voice came from behind me. I turned to see her and Dr Silk stepping through a door in the far wall which wasn't there before. I hated places with secret passageways and rooms. Why couldn't everything be out in the open and genuine?

I dropped a crust on to the table and pulled a stray piece of lettuce from my teeth. 'Thanks, Mum.'

It was the first time I'd used that term with her and it

had an immediate effect: she beamed brighter than the sun while her eyes lit up like fireworks.

'We have a gift for you, Alice.'

She and Dr Silk approached me, and I noticed she carried something in her hands. I swallowed the last of the food and stood. She unfurled what she had: it was a white lab coat, all shiny and new, with my name stitched into the front.

Crumbs dropped from my lips. 'What's this?'

Mother threw her arms around me. My reservations about personal contact evaporated and I gave her the embrace I'd been waiting for all my life. She kissed me on the forehead, and then pulled away. She thrust the lab coat into my trembling hands.

'Julius and I discussed this last night when you were out.' She glanced at him. 'And we've put all the resources of the Foundation at your disposal to explore and develop the theory you mentioned yesterday.'

The material was smooth between my fingers, its cleanliness contrasting with the fog in my head.

'What do you mean?'

'Come with me; it will be easier to show you.' She took my free hand and led me towards the secret door she'd emerged from. Dr Silk and Amy went in before us.

We entered the annexe. I expected it to be smaller than the previous room, but it was twice the size. I'd been inside a few labs at university, but never one this big. There was everything you'd expect to see in a working laboratory: safety goggles and equipment, beakers, flasks, test tubes, cylinders, ring stands, rings, and clamps, tongs, forceps, and spatulas.

And there were plenty of white-coated people using the paraphernalia, but what attracted my gaze were a few familiar faces from yesterday. They sat together, the three supernatural teenagers, at a table, peering into their phones, the winged girl hovering a few feet above the others. She glanced over and smiled at me when she realised I was there. To the right of them stood Grace, not in her troll form now, talking animatedly to a member of the Foundation.

But they weren't the only supernatural beings in the room. I stepped forward, past the others, and stared transfixed at the group before me: four people who were not people in the human sense of the word. The closest one approached me. Her face comprised a swarm of bees as they buzzed and vibrated underneath her shock of ruby hair. The two largest insects parted in the middle to reveal soft yellow eyes, one below for the nose and another batch for her mouth. Her voice was like velvet honey.

'Hi there, Alice.' She held out her hand, which, thankfully, wasn't covered in bees. 'My name is Melissa.'

I shook her hand, my mind swirling as much as the bees did in the space where her face should have been. Their wings picked up speed and fluttered in a frenzy before every one of them sank back into Melissa's head and were replaced by human flesh.

'That's amazing.' I'd seen a lot of strange things recently, but that had to take the biscuit.

Melissa continued to grin at me. She smelt of sugar and sweetness, and it made me giddy.

'I'm a Thriae, sometimes called a bee maiden.'

'Be careful of Melissa.' A tall, skinny youth stepped forward and thrust his bony fingers towards me. 'She can make people tell the truth.'

Melissa laughed, and two giant bees flew from her mouth and up to the ceiling. 'Now, Sandy, you know that's not true.' She grinned while the boy, Sandy, took my hand.

His grip was stronger than he looked. When his skin touched mine, my legs trembled and sudden tiredness swept through me. Melissa dragged us apart.

'He's the one you've got to watch out for, Alice; he's a sandboy, desperate to be a sandman.'

I staggered back a little, my senses working overtime to adjust to this, and I bumped into another teenage boy. He had a rose in one hand. His olive skin matched his eyes, from which a fierce honesty shone. His hair was long, dark and luscious as it hung to his shoulders. But none of that was what held my gaze; he had no mouth.

It was Melissa who spoke. 'Alice, this is Astomi.'

Astomi handed the flower to me and I took it. Melissa whispered into my ear. 'I think he likes you.'

The beat of my heart doubled its normal speed and a jolting heat spread through my cheeks. The only thing which stopped me from bursting into flames were the cold female fingers that grabbed my free hand. I gazed up into beautiful green eyes with a single dot of white in the middle of them.

'I'm Yuki-Onna.'

She continued to hold on to me, this stunning Japanese girl. If Astomi's hair was long, it was nothing compared to Yuki-Onna's, which was snow white and reached the floor. There was so much of it, I wondered how she could walk.

'This is how it all starts, Alice.'

My mother approached us and the others moved back a little in deference. My world was spinning, and I needed to sit down. I ignored the confusion and faced her.

'This is how what starts, Mother?'

Dr Silk had come with her and she looked at him. Then she held her hands out wide, as if trying to snatch the whole of the room into her grasp.

'It's all about you, Alice.' Her smile made my eyes hurt. 'This is your project and you will be our Darwin.'

My brain was inside a hyperactive washing machine. 'You're not making any sense, Mother.'

She placed her palm on the lab coat in my hand, her fingers touching the stitching of my name.

'Today, Alice, under your leadership, we start working on your theory of the evolution of species, the evolution of the supernatural.'

It was at that point my legs gave way.

14 CASSIE: MAGICAL MYSTERY TOUR

I pushed at the haze, trying to see what was around me, but there was nothing apart from the chilled sea breeze. 'Are you there, Vika?'

The silence was the only reply. That and the thumping of my heart against my ribs and echoing inside my skull. It wasn't just Pandora's blue mist in Valhalla this reminded me of, but also the time Alice and I went to Limbo. The fog engulfing me now was similar to that, and then we were attacked by a group of harpies. Was that what Vika had seen above us before the vapour had descended?

I clenched my hands into fists, legs braced for an attack as I peered above me. There was something there. I was sure of it, even though all I saw was the thick fog. My eyes were narrowing to get used to the dense haze when some-one's mobile ringtone went off.

Let's Dance by David Bowie cut through the air as I moved my arms like a windmill, forcing the mist away until it vanished as quickly as it had appeared. I could see the world around me now, and Vika had the phone to her ear as she whispered something I couldn't hear.

I twisted my neck to peer into the sky, searching for the thing she'd thought she'd seen before the fog had descended: all I saw was a dark sky and a full moon hanging over my head.

Vika stepped towards me. 'That was Susan Saxon, asking to speak to her husband.'

'Did you tell her we haven't got to the house yet?'

The vampire nodded. 'She was on her way to bed.'

'Couldn't she have called him directly?'

She put the phone into her jacket. 'I don't allow any electronic devices into the Impossible Palace or any calls out of there.' She peered into the sky at what might have been a shooting star, but was probably a satellite. 'You never know who is watching and listening.'

I didn't reply and moved towards the whalebone arch, standing beneath the twenty-foot jawbones and gazing out to the sea.

'Well, at least there are no cameras attached to these bones.' I placed one hand on them and imagined the whale living free in the ocean.

Vika joined me. 'Do you know the history of this arch?'

I shook my head. 'I'd guess it involves a lot of death.'

She laughed at me. 'Doesn't everything in this world?' Vika moved from underneath the bones. 'Whaling was a chance for great wealth for those who managed a successful catch, but incredibly dangerous. The elements and the whales sometimes capsized a boat in an instant, killing many men. On a fleet's return to port, eager onlookers would watch for the telltale sign of good news: crews would tie a whale's jaw bone atop the ship's mast as a signal they'd killed the mammal and not the other way around. To recognise this tradition and Whitby's important whaling history, the town erected a whalebone arch here in the middle of the nineteenth century.' She came towards me and put her fingers on the bone. 'These are not the original bones, but they are a timely warning to those setting out to tame the great beasts of this fragile planet.' Vika removed her hand and placed it on her wounded hip. She stared at me. 'You and your sister may have prevented a nuclear Armageddon, but I've tasted the maggots in the human mind and I often wonder how long this world has left.'

I didn't know what to say to her, so I turned away and looked for the Saxon residence. I'd wanted to get out of the Impossible Palace to try to help Vika out of her funk, but the opposite seemed to be happening. So I thought I might as well do what I'd promised Susan Saxon and let her husband know she was okay.

'That must be the Saxon house there.' I pointed across the street at the place matching the address Susan had given us. 'But it looks like a bed-and-breakfast joint.' Could the Saxons be renting a room there?

Vika crossed the road with me. 'Most places around here are guest houses for the tourist trade. So this must be another one.'

I rechecked the paper to ensure we had the correct address before walking up to knock on the door.

'What should we say about his wife? We can't exactly tell him about the Impossible Palace, can we?'

She laughed. 'It would be funny to see his reaction, though.'

As I was about to bang on the entrance, I noticed the twitching curtains in the upstairs window. Then the door opened before I could touch it. Standing there was a woman in her thirties, smiling at us through crooked teeth.

'Are you here for John?'

I nodded. 'John Saxon, yes. We have a message for him from his wife.'

She clapped her hands together. 'Oh, Susan. Is she okay?'

'Yes,' I said. 'Is John here? Can we speak to him?'

Vika stared at her fingernails, seemingly bored. 'Or you can just give him a message from us.'

The woman shook her head. 'Oh no, you must come through. He'll want to hear this from you.'

She moved inside without waiting for us or to close the door. I did that as we followed her down a dark, narrow passage and into a large living room. I turned up my nose at the smell, which resembled what you'd find at the bottom of a dumpster truck. Vika stared at the walls covered with stuffed animal heads. If the building was a guest house, I assumed it would only attract a limited range of clients. It was sparse in furniture, with a couple of two-seater sofas and some chairs. The woman indicted for us to sit down and we took seats opposite each other.

'Thank you,' I said.

'Would you like tea and biscuits while you wait for John?'

I nodded. 'Yes, that would be great.'

Vika shook her head. 'Do you have anything stronger? Whisky with ice and water will suffice.'

The woman thought about it for a second. 'I'll see what I can do.' Then she left us alone.

Vika crossed her legs and gazed at her fingers again. 'I'm guessing this isn't one of the five-star establishments in the town.'

I tried to ignore the dead eyes of the animal heads above us. 'Perhaps you should open up the Impossible Palace as a bed-and-breakfast place.'

She laughed. 'I think I already have.'

Vika's enjoyment made me feel good and I relaxed into the chair as the woman returned with the refreshments. She pushed a trolley up to my legs. On it was a pot of tea, a plate of chocolate biscuits, jugs of water and milk, sugar cubes, and an unopened bottle of whisky.

'John will see you soon,' she said before leaving us again.

Vika grabbed the bottle and gave herself a generous measure. 'It was worth coming out tonight after all.' She waved the bottle at me. 'Would you like some?'

I poured milk and tea into a cup and narrowed my eyes at her. 'I'm sixteen years old.'

She downed her drink before pouring another one. 'Come on, Cassie, don't tell me you haven't had alcohol before.'

I bit through a biscuit and sipped at the tea, expecting it to be too hot. It wasn't, so I drank half of it.

'You're a bad influence, Vika Vistala.'

She grinned at me. 'You might be right, Cassandra Arcane.' She grabbed two sugar cubes and ate them as if they were the last food on Earth. I was about to reply when a man came into the room.

'Hi.' He held out his hand. 'I'm Dr John Saxon. Carol tells me you have news about my wife, Susan.'

Vika didn't move, so I shook his hand as he stood between us, reaching up to feel the heat coming off his skin. His short grey hair looked as if he'd just come from the barber's, standing up on his head like small electric pylons. His eyes were narrow and brown, seemingly out of place on a face as large as a dinner plate.

'You're a doctor?' I said as I let go of his hand and wiped mine on my trouser leg.

His face moved up and down like an overexcited

nodding dog. 'Indeed. I am a purveyor of exotic medicines. I studied in Glasgow and London while serving as a surgeon's mate on ships trading with African ports. I've travelled throughout Europe, Africa and America, eventually settling in Newcastle where I met Susan.'

I finished the tea and wondered why my mouth was dry. 'Susan told us she'd left a cult, the Church of the Eternal Light. Are you aware of them?'

Saxon rubbed his chin. 'The mind is like a foreign land, unmapped territory whose distant currents and eddies we only dimly perceive.'

I went to speak, but my lips wouldn't move. Then, as I tried to raise my arm, everything moved around me in slow motion. Saxon was out of his seat, moving towards Vika as she lifted the glass to her face, so had her view of him obscured. My vision was blurred; finding it difficult to see what was in his hand, I knew something was there: sharp and wooden.

As the words refused to leave my throat in a vain attempt to warn Vika, he leapt forward and thrust the stake straight between her ribs and into her heart.

The glass fell from her hand and bounced off the carpet to roll at my feet. The whisky stained my shoes as Vika's flesh crumbled from her body: first, it was the skin around her fingers that withered and flaked into nothing, followed by the collapse of her face. Next, her cheeks sank away as her eyes disappeared along with her hair. Even in my frozen state, I heard the scream before her lips vanished and all that remained of my vampire companion was a skull and bones inside her clothes.

Saxon grinned at me. 'We thought the vamp would never get here.' He reached out a hand and ran his fingers over my cheek. The bile got stuck in my unmoving throat and I thought I'd choke. 'You must be one of her little helpers.' My eyes bulged as I struggled to breathe. Then he slapped me on the back and the vomit slipped into my guts. 'Still, we can't have you dying on us.' He rubbed his thumb along the length of my spine. 'We can never have too many sacrifices for the Ageless Ones.'

Two young women wearing purple robes entered the room carrying a tarpaulin.

'Shall we take the vampire downstairs?' the taller said.

Saxon removed his hand from my back. 'Be very careful with her, Jeanie. If that stake comes out before we need it to, she'll kill us all.' He ran his fingers through my hair. 'It doesn't matter about this one. Once the drug wears off and she can move again, we'll drain her ready for the transference to the Ageless realm.'

Jeanie nodded as she and her partner placed the tarpaulin on the floor and carefully moved Vika's remains to it. My brain was as numb as the rest of me, but I still searched for my Arcane abilities, looking for the telekinesis to work so I could pull the stake from Vika's chest.

But nothing came and all I could do was watch them bundle Vika's bones up.

'Will we send her through the dimensional door tonight as we did with the other vamps?' Jeanie said.

Saxon took the seat opposite me and poured himself a shot of whisky. 'Yes, we will. With this one, that will be eight we've given over to the Ageless Ones, and that should be enough for one of them to make the journey to our world.'

Jeanie's companion spoke. 'But without your wife, we don't have a vessel for it.'

He sipped at his glass. 'Yes. Susan will eventually pay for her betrayal, but for now, I think we have an adequate replacement to host the first Ageless One to come here in a hundred thousand years. She hasn't had the training and the preparation my wife has, but her youth should be enough to contain the form of the Ageless One.' He grinned at me. 'It will be an endless agonising pain for her, but we all have sacrifices to make.'

Saxon raised the glass to me and I wished I'd choked on that bile.

15 ALICE: BLOOD

I didn't fall, but placed my hand on my mother's and steadied my feet.

'The evolution of the supernatural?'

She led me towards the groups of white-coated people working in the lab.

'Ever since I created the Foundation - long before your father betrayed me, betrayed us, and Lucy dragged me to Hell – I've wanted to help others like me. It didn't matter if they were human or supernatural. After centuries of running and hiding, I was determined to support the oppressed of this world. But I was never sure how to go about it. The organisation was in its earliest stages when I went into hospital and...' She stared at me. 'Well, you know the rest.'

Dr Silk was at my side. 'I did my best without your mother's guidance, helping the less fortunate in the city where I could, but it was always difficult reaching out to those beings that weren't human.' He beamed at her, and then at me. 'But now, with you two here, we can fulfil all of our ambitions.'

Mother led me to a bench full of test tubes and phials. 'Julius and his colleagues will collect blood and DNA samples from every supernatural being we find.' She pointed at Amy. 'Ms Weaver has been promoted to oversee all the data collecting, inputting, and collating. And you, my dear daughter, will analyse everything we gather and formulate a system of the supernatural to rival Darwin's theory of evolution of natural species.'

My legs buckled again, and this time I had to grab a seat. 'I need a drink.'

With shaky fingers, I grabbed hold of the bench, the plastic cold to my touch.

'Here you are, Alice.'

Amy was at my side with a glass of water. I took it and downed it. It slipped between my lips and shivered against the back of my throat. I finished it and placed the glass next to a test tube full of red liquid. It was sealed, but I knew if I removed the stopper, I'd smell blood.

I steadied the shakes and looked around the annexe, observing the people at work and the supernatural creatures I'd just met. To be a scientist; to run experiments, discover new things, and change the world: that's all I'd wanted since forever. And now everything was waiting for me.

My mother beamed at me. No, that wasn't all I'd wanted. I'd desired a family as well: a real family, not those fake ones who pretended to like me in all those care homes and foster houses. Well, now I had one. I smiled back at her. It was only when I clenched my fists I remembered I had a sister.

Or did I still have a sister? If what Mother had told me last night was true, would I feel the same way about Cassie if she was working for the American government?

'So, what do you think?' Mother's hand was on my shoulder. I placed my fingers on hers.

'This is wonderful; thank you.' Our smiles mirrored each other's. 'This is a dream come true for me, but we need to change the terminology we use before we begin.'

She pulled up a seat opposite. 'What do you mean?'

I looked over at the group I'd recently been introduced to, still marvelling at Melissa's bees, Sandy's sleep-inducing touch, the mouthless Astomi, and the cold beauty of Yuki-Onna.

'These are real people, Mother. They may be of the supernatural, but they're not creatures or monsters; they're people as much as any human.'

She nodded and looked at me as if she was the proudest parent in the world. 'You're right, Alice: you, me, and all of them, we're supernatural people, and today is the first step in recording all of our community.' She gripped my fingers. 'You're about to lead the greatest scientific project in history, both human and supernatural.'

The pride seeped out of her and into me, delivering a joy I'd never felt before. But there was still one thing we had to deal with.

'What about Cassie? Do you have more news?'

Mother let go of my fingers, the excitement in her face disappearing, replaced with a sadness which made her shoulders slump and her back arch.

'Julius continues to reach out to his contacts, but there's nothing more than what I told you last night.'

'I can't believe Cassie would work for any government or official organisation.'

My mother crossed her legs and placed her hands on her knees. 'I agree, Alice, but we need more information from the States before we do anything; we don't even know where your sister is at this moment.'

I glanced around the lab. 'Do we know of any supernaturals who can locate people, maybe with a spell or a vision?' How quickly I'd slipped into a world where everything was possible.

'Including those in this room, and us, there are less than a dozen supernaturals within the Foundation. Once we gather material and talk to others, we'll hopefully find someone to help us in the search for Cassie.' Her shoulders slumped again. 'For now, all we can do is wait.'

The chair creaked under me as I jumped out of it. 'At least all this will keep me busy.' Cassie's image slipped into the shadows of my mind and I tried to ignore the guilt.

My mother followed me from the bench. 'So, where do you want to start?'

The blood; everything started with the blood.

'Have you taken samples from all the supernaturals in this room?'

'Well, not everyone.' She stared right at me.

'You mean me?'

'And me.'

'Okay; let's make a comparison now.' I marched to where Dr Silk was speaking to Amy. 'Get some syringes, Doc; you'll take some samples.' A smile spread across his face as if he'd won the lottery. I rolled up my sleeve and pointed at my mother and then Amy. 'You two do the same as me.'

A nervous tic made Amy's eyelids flicker faster than usual. 'Am I going to be a guinea pig?' She tried to make light of it, but the tremble in her voice told me otherwise.

'What's wrong, Amy?'

'If you put a needle in me, I'll faint.' She looked sheep-ish. 'It's a phobia I've had since childhood.'

She couldn't hide the fear in her eyes.

'Don't worry; we'll use Dr Silk's blood instead.'

He returned with three new syringes. Then he used them to get samples from me, himself, and my mother. He squeezed the blood into individual Petri dishes. Amy breathed a sigh of relief as Silk pushed his sample underneath a microscope. I expected us to take turns peering at it, but he tripped a switch on the side and a display appeared on an enormous screen on the bench.

'I can transfer the data from each sample into the database, and then get the computer to analyse them,' he said. 'We can also observe them side-by-side on the monitor.'

Mother was suitably impressed. 'The world has changed while I've been away.'

There was a curious stare in Amy's eyes, which made me think she was too shy to ask where my mother had been these last sixteen years. I was in no rush to tell her about the existence of Hell.

Dr Silk placed each sample under the microscope and got the machines to do their work. Then he displayed the information on the monitor one at a time, starting with his. He joked when his name came up on the computer.

'I hope it finds nothing wrong with me.'

My mother patted him on the shoulder. 'Don't worry, Julius, everything looks fine.'

Amy leant in to get a closer look. 'How do you know which cells are which?' Dr Silk was about to answer when I butted in.

'Red blood cells transport respiratory gases, oxygen and carbon dioxide, while the white ones provide defence mechanisms for fighting foreign microorganisms entering the human organism.' This was one of the first things I'd taught myself as a kid, right after I'd cut myself on a piece of glass. 'Red blood cells are red, hence their name. The colour is made because of haemoglobin. White blood cells are colourless. The blood also contains plasma and platelets.'

Fascination rippled through Amy's face. 'What do those do?'

I dug deep into my medical knowledge. 'The main job of the plasma is to transport blood cells throughout the body, along with nutrients, waste products, antibodies, clotting proteins, chemical messengers such as hormones, and proteins which maintain the body's fluid balance. In addition, platelets help the blood clotting process by gathering at an injury, sticking to the lining of the injured blood vessel, and forming a platform on which blood coagulation can occur.' I felt like a scientist again, admittedly as a sixteen-year-old girl who'd completed none of her science exams since leaving school. But I'd studied enough.

'That's excellent, Alice; now let's have a look at your blood.' Silk changed the display and my name popped up. There didn't appear to be any difference between mine and his.

'It's the same.' Amy sounded disappointed.

My mother pointed at the screen. 'No, it isn't. Can you magnify that spot, Julius?'

He pressed a button and the image increased. The cells we'd scrutinised for his sample were different; around mine, white or red, was a slim circular line of green luminescence. It was as if someone had taken a crayon and drawn a thin mark of lime around the life inside me.

Silk scratched his head. 'That is an unusual colour, plus the nucleus is larger and darker than normal, almost as if...'

Why was I not surprised my blood was different? 'It's almost as if what, Doctor?'

There was strain on his face as he replied. 'A larger and darker nucleus is one of the physical characteristics of cancer cells.'

Well, that was great news. 'But not that green luminescence around the cells; that isn't a sign of cancer?'

'There are no cancer cells like that which I'm aware of.' He increased the magnification on the screen again. 'You have more cells like that mixed in with the red and white.' He appeared to do a quick count as I analysed the image. 'There's maybe one with a green hue for every half a dozen of the standard ones.'

'Let's see what my mother's blood is like.'

Dr Silk added her data next to his and mine, zooming in to get a more detailed look. 'You have the same cells as your daughter, Mary, but not the same amount; perhaps half as many as she has.' He appeared to ponder this discovery of a new blood cell. 'It will be interesting to see what we discover from the other supernatural people we have here.'

I turned from the screen. 'I'm curious to compare our DNA, but I'd guess that's a long process.'

The doctor nodded. 'You are correct, Alice.'

My mother placed her hand on mine. I stared at it, an image in my mind of those cells with the green luminescence flowing through our veins. She leant in close to my ear.

'I've got some other news.'

'Is it about Cassie?'

'Yes, but it's not good.'

My heart appeared to halt, those curious cells freezing inside my blood.

'What's happened?' My lips trembled against each other.

'It's best if I show you; follow me.' She led me from Amy and the doctor, down by the equipment and the others in the laboratory. The winged girl floated above the main table and winked at me.

We left the annexe by a different way from which I'd entered, heading down a corridor and into a lift at the far end.

'Where are we going?'

She pressed a button for the top floor. 'Julius gave me the best room in the building. It's not exactly a penthouse, but more luxury than I've had in a long time.' She appeared to have forgotten about her missing daughter. 'You can stay there with me; it has two bedrooms.'

We travelled up in silence. No news was good news.

The lift stopped and we exited into another corridor. There was only one room at the end. She opened the door and we went inside. It was the same as the room as I had, only three times the size. She walked over to a large laptop sitting on a desk. It was switched on with the screen frozen on an image of Cassie.

I ran to it. 'What is this?'

'Julius's contacts sent it to him a few hours ago.' Sadness filled her eyes. 'I've watched it twice. I have to warn you, Alice; it's hard viewing.'

I didn't care. I had to find out what had happened to my sister.

'Play it.'

16 CASSIE: CHURCH OF THE POISON MIND

I knew as they carried me downstairs, they meant to kill me.

They dumped me in the corner, straight on to the floor. I slumped against the wall as the rats ran from me.

'The Church of the Eternal Light is not a cult, young lady.'

John Saxon stood opposite me, watching as the two women who'd brought me down joined four others in the basement. Apart from Saxon, they all wore the same purple robes. Movement returned to my face as they scrutinised me.

'You look like a cult to me.'

He pulled up a chair next to me as the others got busy doing something in the far shadows.

'How old are you, sixteen?' His eyes peered right through me. 'You'll be the youngest we've bled for the Ageless Ones. I think they'll enjoy that.'

'I thought you said I was going to be the host for one of these creatures?'

Saxon nodded. 'Indeed, which is why we won't bleed you dry as we've done with the other humans. It will be just enough to give them a taste, and then the first one will be able to adapt to your physiology without too many teething problems.'

My tongue touched the side of my mouth, but I felt nothing. 'Who are these Ageless Ones? I'd like to know more about them if one is going to cohabitate with me inside my skin.'

He laughed. 'Oh, dear girl, there'll be no cohabitation. Once the Ageless One possesses your body, it will slowly consume you from the inside. Your mind will die a thousand deaths every day. You'll have no control of anything as you cry out for the release of death, which might come soon, or it may arrive years from now. It depends on whether the creature wants you there as amusement.'

'How do you know all this, Saxon? What are these creatures? Are they demons?'

That's what they sounded like to me. Demons and angels crawled inside a human and used it as a vessel. For angels, according to my father, the human host had to give up their body willingly. Whereas demons just took what they wanted.

He scowled at me. 'Demons are foul beasts, the evil offspring of Satan. The Ageless Ones are much purer than that. They exist in another dimension to ours, not some unholy place for God's cast-offs.'

'So I'll ask again: how do you know this? I mean, no offence, Saxon, but you don't appear to be the brightest bulb in the ceiling.'

I'd hoped my little insult would force him to strike me, to knock some life back into my body so it wasn't only my mouth I could move. But he didn't fall for the bait.

'You didn't believe me earlier when I told you I'm a doctor, did you?'

'I wouldn't trust you to prescribe me painkillers, Saxon.'

His scowl turned into a grin. 'You'll be begging me for them later, I promise you.'

I tried to shrug, but my shoulders wouldn't budge. 'Since you're not answering my question, I'm guessing you stumbled into all this nonsense, or you stole it from someone else. Did you join the cult, and then oust the leadership to take over?'

He leant closer to me. 'How old do you think I am, girl?'

'My name is Cassie, and looking at the lines on your face, I'd say you're fifty.'

He looked about thirty, but I was trying to bait him into violence again. Once more, it didn't work.

'I'm three hundred years old, Cassie. I discovered an ancient tome a long time ago that led me to the gaps between dimensions and the Old Gods existing in these realms. Would you like to see a doorway to another world?'

He spoke to me as if I was a teenager struggling with homework and unrequited love, not someone whose footsteps lingered in Hell, Heaven, Purgatory and Limbo. I hoped his ignorance would be his undoing, and I could resurrect Vika.

'Anything would be better than listening to your voice.'

He turned from me and called to his acolytes. 'Jeanie and Eric, come here and take the host to the doorway.'

They did as he instructed, grabbing my arms and dragging me to the back of the basement. The rats scampered before us, with my feet kicking up dust and dirt. Saxon's people carried me forward before dropping me to the ground. I could move just enough to roll over, finding my head next to Vika's bones. I wanted to crawl to her to grab the stake, but it was impossible.

And then I saw the shimmering gap near me.

A golden light cut through the air in front of me, reminiscent of the shape my friend Kai, the Warwitch, had created when using the Blade of Reality to cross between different parts of the world. Was that what Saxon had used to reach this realm of the so-called Ageless Ones? I'd lost the Blade of Reality weeks ago in Newcastle when the police had tried to arrest Alice and me.

'What is that?' I said.

Saxon loomed over me. 'That is a doorway to an ancient dimension. The Church of the Eternal Light passes offerings of blood and flesh through there, and we receive gifts in return. Vampire blood is the most desired by the Ageless Ones, and for that offering, they provide my followers and me with the Eternal Light, the elixir of immortality.'

I watched him licking his lips with glee and understood what he meant.

'You send them vampire and human blood, and they return the gesture, right?'

He touched my hair and I cringed. 'We give them the bodies, but it's the blood they desire. And we get these in return.'

Saxon stood and went into the shadows. When he returned, he showed me what was in his hands: eggs, large enough to have come from an ostrich.

My guts churned at the sight. 'Are they what I think they are?'

He nodded. 'These are the seeds of the Ageless Ones, and they confer immortality on those who eat them regularly.'

I wanted to throw up, but my stomach refused to move. 'And that's what you've been doing?'

Saxon's eyes sparkled. 'And once an Ageless One takes your body as its vessel, you'll provide offspring much more valuable than these small eggs.'

There was no stopping it this time as I jerked to the side and vomited all over the place. It happened twice more before I could lift and wipe the spew from my face. I hadn't regained full movement, but it was improving. All I had to do was get the stake out of Vika's chest and we could deal with these fanatics.

'I'm not surprised your wife fled from you, Saxon.'

He put the two eggs on the ground and smiled at me. 'Unfortunately, Susan was never strong enough for this project, but I've always known where she was in this town.' He glanced at Vika's bones. 'Our spies knew the vampire was somewhere in the Abbey and it would only be a matter of time before we had her in our control. So it was nice of the both of you to come straight here.'

'Are you the ones who attacked her near the skate park?'

Saxon narrowed his eyes. 'No, that wasn't us. There are many forces at work in the world now, Cassie. It could have been anyone.'

Did I believe him? I suppose I had no choice. 'What will you do with Vika?'

He turned to glance at her. 'We will remove the stake from her heart and roll her through the doorway. Then we'll prepare for the Ageless One to enter your body.'

'You've read about this in a book somewhere, this process, haven't you?'

'It's an ancient procedure, well documented through the ages. So there should be no problems, but if it comes to the worst, you'll still be dead.'

He waved his hand at the group behind him. The woman, Jeanie, came over and handed him a knife.

I flexed my fingers and wondered if I had the strength to defeat all of them. 'If you're making something to eat, I'll have a burger and fries.'

Saxon ran his hand over the blade. 'The only food here will be you and the vampire.'

Before I could reply, two of his cult got behind me and grabbed my arms. My movement was returning, but not enough to shake them off.

'What if it all goes wrong, Saxon, and this Ageless One kills you and the rest of your thugs?'

He shook his head and placed the knife close to my wrist. 'In your desperation, you twist your words to make us doubt the purity of our task, but it won't work, girl. The Church of Eternal Light exists because I do, and I've prepared for this moment for three hundred years.'

As he droned on, I reached into my mind. He was right. I was desperate, searching for my Arcane abilities deep inside me. I closed my eyes and blocked out everything around me, picturing these people flying from me and smashing into the walls.

Nothing happened.

So I tried again, picturing myself outside the building, across the other side of the town and back to the Impossible Palace.

It didn't happen.

My eyes flicked open as Saxon cut across my wrist. The blood dripped out of me and my energy went at the same time. I glanced down, seeing the liquid dripping into a bowl held there by Jeanie.

'I'll kill you when I get free, Saxon.'

He grinned and wiped the blade over my cheek. 'I

wonder how much of you will still be in there when I mate with the Ageless One possessing your body.'

I yelled and waited for the Arcane to return.

It didn't.

But I felt a breeze blow across the room as if somebody had opened the door into the basement.

Then others screamed.

It was the men holding me. They shrieked once before their heads fell from their shoulders. They dropped at my feet with eyes gazing at me.

Jeanie was next. I saw the fear in her face before I noticed the blood gushing from her throat. She held up a hand before collapsing into the dirt.

What happened then was a blur. A whirlwind erupted in front of me while the rest of Saxon's acolytes screamed as they were ripped open. It must have lasted no more than thirty seconds before everyone in that basement apart from Saxon and me was dead.

And one more.

'This is a terrible fancy dress party, Cassie.'

She reached down to help me up and I took her hand.

'This is why you're my best friend, Claudia.'

Claudia laughed as she pulled me up. 'I think I'm your only friend.' She glanced behind her. 'But what do you want to do with him? I could have killed him, but thought you might like that pleasure.'

I stood next to Claudia and stared at Saxon. 'He claims to be immortal. Perhaps we should bury him alive and leave him like that.'

He glared at me, his face a mixture of fury and fear. The strength had returned to my legs and I stepped towards him. Then he grinned at me before jumping through the doorway into the realm of the Ageless Ones.

Claudia let out a long whistle. 'Where does that go to?'

I gave her a potted history of what he'd told me about the Ageless Ones. Then I pointed at the eggs left behind.

'That's what he ate to gain immortality, so he claimed.'

Claudia grimaced. 'That's sick. What will we do with them and this doorway? If any of what he said is true, we can't leave that open.'

I was thinking of an answer and coming up with nothing when the doorway closed itself and vanished.

'Okay, that's one problem solved. We could smash the eggs.'

'Who is that?' Claudia pointed at Vika's bones.

I told her. 'She's been helping me.'

'Cool,' Claudia said before she reached down and removed the stake in Vika's heart.

The resurrection was instantaneous. Muscle and blood returned life to Vika in a flash. Before I could do anything, she leapt into the air and flew at Claudia.

The two vampires crashed to the ground and rolled through the dirt. Vika hissed at Claudia as she tried to rip out her throat. But my friend had the greater leverage and hurled Vika against the far wall.

'Stop this, Vika,' I shouted. 'She's my friend and she saved us tonight.'

Vika dusted herself down and placed a hand over her heart. 'That was a terrible experience. Was it Susan's husband who did all this?'

I nodded and gave her a short history of the night's events. Then I turned to Claudia.

'How did you find me?' The sight of her lifted my spirits.

'That's a long story, Cassie.' She glanced at Vika. 'Once you convince her I'm not the enemy.'

Vika laughed. 'I'm no threat to you, little vampire. But how did you find us?'

Claudia looked at me. 'Olivia Erasmus told me where you were before I left Valhalla, and it wasn't the only thing she said.'

'What do you mean?'

'She told me where your mother and your sister were.'

That's when my heart went into overdrive.

17 ALICE: RESEARCH

My reflection stared at me from the screen. Then it moved while I stood transfixed. Only it wasn't me, but Cassie, striding through an unknown land as my mother played the video.

There was no sound. She looked exactly as I'd seen her last, only wearing different clothes: black trousers and top, plus dark gloves. There must have been someone with her, the person filming, and they got the camera close to Cassie's face before I saw the missing part of her ear. I wanted to reach out and touch it, my hand trembling to match the irregular beat of my heart.

She walked through a landscape strewn with rubble, damaged buildings on either side of her. Smoke and dust were everywhere, but they weren't enough to block out the harsh light of a low-hanging sun.

'Do we know where this is?'

'Julius was told it's somewhere in the Middle East.'

An emaciated camel strode into view to confirm that, not even looking at Cassie as it disappeared off camera. My sister and her companion continued to walk on for another two minutes, moving past craters of rubble and what looked like the shells from exploded bombs. Dust lingered in the air and drifted towards the screen, and I thought I could smell burning near me. Then Cassie lifted her hand and stopped dead.

My mother paused the clip. 'Are you sure you want to continue watching, Alice?' Her face swam with concern, her eyes narrowing and her lips shaking a little.

'I have to see it.'

She started it again. The ground shook in front of Cassie, the sand swirling around her, grains of it bubbling and bouncing into the air. She took two steps back. My fingers trembled as much as the environment did. Something rose from the sand, a vast bulk that must have been seven or eight feet tall. It was reminiscent of the trolls I'd fought last night, but it was larger, more muscular. It had the face of a gargoyle, yellow eyes burning in its skull. Its hands were as big as shovels, with nails long and sharp enough to rip off a head with one movement.

Its shadow inched towards my sister until it covered her. Nothing moved and I thought the clip had frozen, just like my heart had. Then the creature lifted a hand and brought it crashing down on Cassie's head. I clutched at my face and gasped. Only Cassie wasn't there anymore; none of her was. Instead, she reappeared floating above the beast and wrapped her legs around its throat. The camera wobbled as the gargoyle thrashed about, its long grey fingers reaching up to Cassie, but failing to find her.

She'd vanished again, reappearing at the creature's legs. This time, she had a knife in her hand. Her movement was too quick for me to take in, producing a frenzy of jabbing that stabbed the gargoyle's thighs with what seemed like a thousand strikes. The camera zoomed into the blood seeping from the creature's flesh before moving up to see the agony on its face.

It crashed to the ground, the zoom on the lens catching its anguish in every detail. Its eyes were bulging, vibrating with blood and ready to burst. Its huge hands went to the wounds in its legs, seemingly trying to stop the flow of blood covering the sand. Cassie wasted no time. She took the blade and thrust it into its neck. She must have pushed it in hard enough to force the beast to roll to the side. She moved with it, forcing her knee into its hip and thrusting down even harder with the weapon. In the silence of the room, with my mother near me, I imagined the tortured screams coming from the thing my sister had killed. Then she pulled out the knife and wiped it on her arm.

She turned to the camera and peered straight into it. There was no sign of emotion on her face, no movement in her eyes. Was she drugged?

There was one last view of the body before the lens shifted to the right and focused on a smouldering building. Cassie strode towards it, pushing through the damaged door with no apparent fear or concern. I'd seen her like this before, her mind fixated on the task, so she'd have no awareness of anything else.

She moved inside the structure, with the camera following her. Illumination filtered in through broken windows and a sizeable hole blown through the wall. She stood there, her head glancing from side to side, apparently searching for something. Then, finally, a light appeared from behind her, a torch shining across the room.

'This is the worst part.' My mother sounded on the verge of tears.

I didn't turn to her, but concentrated on the screen.

Something moved from the shadows and into the light. First, there was one, then two, then three, and finally four gargoyles. But these weren't like the one Cassie had killed; one was female, the others were young children.

She'd dealt with the male, and this was the rest of the family.

The light and camera stayed on them. The female said something, tears in her eyes, her hands out pleading. It meant nothing to my sister as she plunged her blade deep into the creature's chest. She repeated it several times before finishing by slicing off the head. I should have stopped watching after she slaughtered the mother, but I couldn't, both horrified and disbelieving of what I'd witnessed. The children tried to crawl from her, their tiny legs fumbling through the dust and the dirt, but finding no escape. The lens panned across each of them, zooming in to their terrified faces before Cassie decapitated the kids one by one, and then held the heads up to the camera.

Then she showed her first sign of emotion: she smiled. I gazed at the mirror image of myself, unbelieving of what I'd seen. Then I remembered what I'd done last night in that house in Leeds, how I'd killed those trolls, and one thought lingered in my head.

We are of the same blood, my sister and I.

The camera cut to black after that.

Against my better judgement, I played it again, this time with my face pressed up to the screen. I scrutinised each pixel, searching for the evidence this wasn't Cassie, but only some elaborate deception. Even in the silence, I heard every scream and listened to each death throe of those children.

An eternity later, the words crawled through my gut and out of my mouth.

'I don't believe any of it. That wasn't Cassie. It must have been an impostor, a shapeshifter.'

Mother turned off the computer and placed her hand on my arm. 'How could she teleport and fly if it was a sham?'

I didn't know. Were there supernaturals that could do those things? I suppose there had to be somewhere. Even if there weren't, it was easy to fake anything on video nowadays.

So I told myself it couldn't have been Cassie. But, deep down, I didn't know.

I looked at my mother to ease my worries. 'Do you think it was her?'

'I've never met her, so I don't know what Cassie is capable of. You know her better than anyone; what do you believe?'

Did I know her? Did I know my sister at all? She was capable of a murderous frenzy, but to kill a mother and her children like that, even if they were gargoyles, was unbelievable to me.

'No, it has to be a fake; something created to discredit her.'

'Or perhaps the Americans brainwashed her into doing this for them.'

Yes, that was possible.

'Why would they send her to the Middle East?'

'There are rumours of terrorist organisations recruiting supernaturals to their cause. Maybe that's why the US government sent Cassie there.'

I pulled away from her and went to the bed. All I wanted to do was bury my head in a pillow and forget everything I'd seen.

'So, what do we do now?'

She sat next to me. 'Julius will continue communicating with his contacts and try to find where she is. Once we know her location, then we can go there and speak to Cassie ourselves. Until then, we'll focus on the work we started today. Your study about the evolution of supernatural species is as important as finding your sister, Alice.' She pointed at the screen where I'd witnessed those horrors. 'We can't let that stop us in our mission.'

My mother was right, but all I thought about was the look on those kids' faces as Cassie, or the fake Cassie, had murdered them one at a time. If I'd had no choice, would I have done that with the trolls last night? There were troll children in that house. I knew that. Would I have killed them if I'd stayed?

'I'll be fine once I've processed this.' The words sounded right, but I didn't believe them.

'Do you want to get your things and stay here with me?'

Did I want that? After years of independence, did I want to run to my mother and hang on to her coattails?

I got off the bed. 'No, I'll stay where I am for now.'

'Okay, Alice; I understand that. What will you do now?'

I had to concentrate on something else. 'Let's head back to the lab and look at the blood of the others.' A scientific study of supernatural people would keep my troubled thoughts at bay, at least for a while.

That's what I hoped.

But when we returned to the lab, it was hard. If I didn't focus on my surroundings, all I saw, everywhere I looked, was Cassie slaughtering those creatures; the images appeared in any piece of glass or computer screen I glanced at, jumped out at me from every mobile phone, and even, at the worst times, danced inside the eyes of those I talked to. It would have been easy to return to my room and bury my head in a pillow, but I didn't. The clip was clearly fake, but I wouldn't let it ruin what was about to begin at the Foundation. I couldn't let such propaganda distract me from what I'd oversee.

I spent the rest of the afternoon getting to know the other supernaturals living within the Foundation. The girl with the tattoos and the wings was a sprite named Sophia. The horned boy was Gregor, a faun, while the girl with the enormous claws was Celestine, who called herself a mormo. Just speaking to them, I knew how fascinating it would be to record and classify as many supernaturals as possible.

With a bit of persuasion, they allowed Amy and me to take samples of their blood. Once we got that under the microscope and into the computer, it was clear to see the subtle differences between their cells and human ones.

Celestine tapped the screen with one of those murderous-looking nails. 'Is this what you mean by the green cells?'

I stared at her and wondered how she'd survived in the world with those claws. 'The cell isn't strictly green, but the outer lining is.' They were the same type as in my and Mother's blood, but there were a lot less of them again, only one or two compared to the dozens I had.

'And all our blood is the same?' Gregor scratched at those horns nearly hidden beneath his hair.

'That's what we've found from our early analysis.' Amy made notes on a digital device as she spoke. 'We need to do more tests to have a greater understanding of how your blood differs from mine, for example.'

Yes, more tests. I'd throw myself into the work and do what I'd always wanted. Whatever had happened to Cassie,

I couldn't do anything until I was better prepared. And the best way of doing that was to discover more about the supernatural world and its inhabitants. Then I'd be able to go to America and find Cassie, see if she was happy in her new life.

Perhaps then we'd both be happy.

18 CASSIE: CLAUDIA

I dragged Claudia towards me. 'Where are they?'

She put her hands on my hips and I got a colossal whiff of jasmine from her hair.

'I know where they were. Olivia Erasmus told me, plus that you were in Whitby.' She glanced at Vika. 'She didn't say you had friends.'

I let go of her, my heart struggling to return to normal. 'Tell me what happened after I left Valhalla.'

'It wasn't long before Olivia and Section 25 arrived: troops, scientists, technicians, medics and doctors. Once she'd made sure her brother was okay, she pulled me, Luke and Colleen into a separate room. I didn't know who was in charge of the operation, but it wasn't her. She allowed the three of us to sneak out of the quarantine zone, but I don't think she was supposed to do that. It was her way of saying thanks for saving her brother, I guess. Plus, she told me where you were before we left and provided details about your mother and sister.'

'What did she say?'

'Section 25 has been sharing information with their British counterparts, AEGIS. It was them who knew your mother and Alice were at Buckingham Palace for a Royal European get-together. There was an incident involving Dracula, and they disappeared after that.'

I placed a hand on my throat and remembered the explosive Section 25 had put there. At least Alice had found our mother. But where were they now?

'Did Erasmus know why they were at Buckingham Palace?'

'She didn't have a lot of time to talk, but she hinted Dracula was working with AEGIS, and it was under their instructions he was there with your mother.'

'Alice must have been there to rescue her.' I went to Vika as she stared at the eggs. 'Have you heard of this government organisation, AEGIS?'

The wind whistled through the basement. 'As you know, I retreated to the Impossible Palace once the threat of the humans starting a nuclear apocalypse seemed likely. From there, and with my contacts, I learnt about the Archangel War, the conflict between Lucy and Michael.' She placed a hand on my shoulder. 'You and your sister stopped the end of everything, but the consequences had serious effects on the supernatural world. Every nation on the planet is probably gathering supernaturals for its own ends. The British have had clandestine organisations investigating the supernatural before. AEGIS is likely the latest one, but I know little about them.'

I understood what she meant. 'Olivia Erasmus told me what happened in America with the creation of Section 25 and the split within its ranks between controlling and imprisoning supernatural creatures or working with them as allies.'

Vika nodded. 'From what I've heard, AEGIS functions on similar lines and, if what your friend says is true, they've already recruited Dracula. That's not good news for anybody.'

Claudia joined in. 'I think they were scared after what you and your sister did, never mind the fact the two of you saved billions of lives. Then Pandora's arrival and her actions exacerbated the problems.'

I stepped back and processed what they'd said. Then I addressed Vika.

'It must be AEGIS operating in Whitby, abducting and killing supernaturals, and across the rest of the country.'

She touched her damaged hip. 'They would seem the only people capable of possessing a weapon which could harm me like that.' She picked the eggs up. 'Especially if it wasn't Saxon and his cult.'

Alice and I had stopped the world from ending, but things had only got worse for us and many others.

'We need to return to the Impossible Palace and get my father awake.'

'Your father?' Claudia spluttered.

'A lot's happened since I saw you last, my friend. I'll fill you in on the way.' We headed upstairs and out of the house. I turned to Vika as we got outside. 'What did you do with the eggs of the Ageless Ones?'

'I smashed them on the ground.'

'Good,' I said. 'What shall we tell Susan Saxon about her husband when we get back?'

Vika shrugged. 'We'll say we couldn't find him. That will do for now.'

It was good enough for me, with my head full of what had happened to Alice and my mother. We made quick time going back, getting there in fewer than fifteen minutes.

The look on Claudia's face as we stepped into the Impossible Palace was a picture, but I had other matters to focus on. I ran to the dining room and got an enormous surprise: Gabriel was sitting with Polyphemus, both stuffing their faces. I went to him.

'Hello, Cassandra.'

There were no big reunion hugs or handshakes, just me frowning at him using my proper name, while inside I beamed. He ate like a man starved of life, munching on a chicken leg as I rambled.

'Are you okay? How did you wake up?'

'I'm fine, Daughter.' He patted his stomach. 'And it's all thanks to Toriyama.'

As he spoke, the monkey appeared from under the table and bowed to me. 'I wriggled through his mind and found his crossed wires. I tied them together, and it was life or death.'

Gabriel smiled at me. 'I chose life.'

'I met George Michael once,' Claudia said beside me. 'He walked into the wrong bathroom at an LA party. So we spent the night getting drunk, and I told him tales of Jim Morrison and Janis Joplin while he repeated a scandalous story about Freddie Mercury and Rod Stewart.'

She grabbed a sandwich from the table while I shook Toriyama's paw and thanked them. I wasn't sure if they were male or female and thought it rude to ask or look too closely. Then it was time to update Gabriel on what I knew about Alice and my mother. He put down his food and got up from his seat.

'You need to know the truth about your mother, Cassie.'

'What do you mean?'

'Perhaps you should hear this in private.'

I looked at Claudia, Vika, and Toriyama. The monkey spoke before I did.

'Don't worry about me; it's time for me to retire.' Toriyama nodded to Vika. 'I'll see you all in the morning.'

I stared at Gabriel. 'I have no secrets from my friends.'

He let out a huge sigh. 'Very well, but you might want to sit down; this isn't easy to hear.'

Vika strode to the table and grabbed a bottle of wine. 'I don't know about you lot, but I need a drink.'

Claudia snatched two glasses. 'That sounds great to me, but none for you, Cassie, since you're too young. How about you, Gabes? Will you have something to keep your throat wet during this talk?'

He looked at me, and then back at her. 'Absolutely.'

Vika led us into the next room: a vast library containing thousands of books; Alice would have loved it. She poured the wine as we sat around a table.

'Susan told me I could store all these volumes and many more on a computer disk, but I said these were unique to this place.' I wasn't in a rush to speak to Susan Saxon, thankful she appeared to have retired for the night. Vika removed a book from a shelf and handed it to me: it was an old copy of *Alice's Adventures in Wonderland*. 'Open it to any page, Cassie.'

I flicked to the middle and everything went black.

When the light returned, I sat at a table with the March Hare, the Hatter, and an exhausted Dormouse. The Hatter yawned and spoke to me.

'Why is a raven like a writing desk?'

Before I could answer, it was dark again, and then I reappeared inside the Impossible Palace with my friends.

'You vanished,' Claudia said. 'Where did you go?'

'I was in the book.' It lay in front of me on the table, closed now. 'I think I was Alice.'

Vika picked it up. 'That's what's so special about these books. Once you open one, you're transported into it as a character.'

I could still smell the aroma of tea in the air. 'And how do you get out?'

'When the book is shut, you return to this world, which is why you need someone with you when opening a volume from this library, or you'll be trapped in the story forever.'

'Does the story change?'

'Not in this reality. From what I can gather, any changes you make create different realities, a new version of that tale.'

'A multiverse of realities,' I said as I peered at the books. 'Alice would love this.'

'Does it work with movies?' Claudia removed something from her pocket and put it on the table; it was a figurine of a woman.

'What's that?' I said.

'It's Ripley from the *Alien* films. I picked it up from a toy shop during my journey to Whitby.' She stared at Vika. 'If it works with movies, I want to try it with *Aliens*. I'd love to be in that film.'

Vika sighed and shook her head. 'No, it only works with the books in this room.'

Gabriel coughed. 'If you're all finished, I'll tell Cassie about her family.' He gazed at me and waited for the silence. 'I'm an archangel, and Mary, your mother, is the last of the Nephilim. Do you know what they were?' I nodded. 'So you understand God sent the Great Flood to destroy the Nephilim, but Mary survived. I was tasked to find and kill her. Instead, we fell in love and hid from God and those searching for her for centuries. They hunted us, so we kept running. Because it was so dangerous, we decided not to have children.'

He took his glass and sipped half of the wine. 'We were both at ease with this, but then things changed and Mary begged me for a family. I refused and thought she was selfish and told her our existence as fugitives was no life for kids, but she wouldn't have it and gave me an ultimatum.'

I scrutinised him and wondered, if he'd had his way, would I be here now? 'What ultimatum?'

'If I didn't give her a child, she'd find someone else who would.' You could hear a pin drop in the library. 'So, I did.' There was a tear in his eye as he stared at me. 'And it was the best thing in my life. But it wasn't long after discovering Mary was pregnant, I knew I'd have to let my babies go.'

The pain in my heart stopped me from asking why. So Claudia did.

'Why did you give them up, Gabriel?'

'I had to when I discovered the real reason Mary wanted children.'

I asked this time. 'What was that?'

He leant over and took my hand. 'She needed your blood, Cassie. From you and your sister when she found out it was twins.'

Daggers flew through my heart. 'Our blood? Why did our mother want our blood?'

'She wanted it for her experiments. Mary planned to use your DNA to create a demon-like army for her revenge on God. That's why I arranged for you and Alice to be taken from the hospital, not because I dreaded Lucy and Michael were after you. On the contrary, I feared what your mother would do, so I organised someone from the Foundation to hide you.'

'The Foundation?' Vika and I said it in unison.

'Mary and I created it to help all those who were scared to be different, for those shunned and hunted by the world. There was a nurse there who I trusted to place you both somewhere safe.' His tears reflected my own. 'You weren't supposed to be separated. I'd arranged to meet her, but she wasn't at the rendezvous, and that's when Seraphiel's spies found me.'

How could this be true? That my mother only wanted me, only wanted Alice, so she could use us for an experiment? No, I wouldn't believe it.

I slammed my fist on the table.

'This is lies!' I stood and grabbed the chair. Molten lava flowed through my veins and exploded into my heart.

Vika got up. 'This Foundation you speak of, where is it based?'

'We didn't want to be in London or somewhere south, so we went north to Leeds.'

'Oh my God!' Vika put a hand to her mouth.

I threw the seat to the ground, still unbelieving at what I'd heard from my father. Maybe he wasn't my father and this was some other trick of Lucy's, or even Michael's. Yes, that had to be it. I couldn't look at him, so focused on Vika.

'What's wrong?'

Vika took the wine bottle and drank straight from it.

'I know I said the Impossible Palace could hold many refugees, but after the first month of letting them in, I knew we'd be overrun if I didn't find sanctuary for them somewhere else. One of my contacts recommended a place in Leeds; it was the Foundation.'

Gabriel wiped his eyes. 'It doesn't matter. Without Mary there, they should be okay.'

I glared at him. 'But she is there, I know it, and so must Alice be.'

And if what he said was true, then my sister was in danger.

If she was still alive.

19 ALICE: TEENAGE KICKS

Six of us went for a day out in Leeds. I wore a hat and dark glasses to make sure nobody would recognise me as a wanted fugitive. Yuki-Onna had tied back her snow-white hair so it hung over her shoulders. I admired her blue lipstick and told her so. She grinned at me.

'It's not lipstick. This is how my lips are all the time. Didn't you notice before?'

'I think Astomi distracted her.' One or two bees were visible inside Melissa's red locks, but the rest of them she'd managed to conceal somewhere.

I scowled at her. 'That's not true.' I blushed as I glanced at Astomi, wishing I was wearing a scarf over my face like he was. He used sign language to speak to Melissa and she giggled. I didn't ask her what he'd said.

Amy stood with Sandy, whispering into his ear. We were outside the Foundation, hanging around like any other group of young people; apart from the fact that, not including Amy, the rest of us were supernaturals.

A small bee crawled down Melissa's nose. 'Can we get some food? I'm starving.'

Amy furrowed her eyebrows. 'Didn't you have breakfast?'

Melissa shook her head. 'None of us did. We were all too excited to be going out after being cooped up for so long.'

I hadn't eaten either, with my worries about Cassie tying my stomach in knots. 'There must be plenty of places in the city centre where we can get food.'

'Mary doesn't want us mingling too much with the locals.' Amy glanced over at everyone. 'We need to keep a low profile while we're out.'

My guts rumbled. 'So what do you suggest?'

She took out her phone. 'I'll order out and we'll go for a picnic.'

Sandy and Yuki-Onna groaned, but the others beamed, especially Melissa.

'Can we visit a park? Then I can let some of the bees out.'

I sidled up to her while Amy checked her mobile. 'Where have you put them?'

She grinned at me and I saw bees fluttering their tiny wings behind her eyes. Then she opened her mouth and there were dozens of them resting at the back of her throat. I didn't know how she managed to speak, but she did.

'They're okay for now, but I'll need to let them out to exercise at some point.'

Amy waved her phone at me. 'Park Square is a ten-minute walk from here. When we get there, I'll order food to be delivered. So everyone needs to think about what they want so we're not wasting any time.'

She sounded like my mother, with that authority in her voice. Then she led us from the Foundation. I walked by her side as we dodged the commuters running into the train station.

'I thought we were going into the city centre,' I said to her as the others gossiped behind us, apart from Astomi, who I noticed looking at me when I glanced over my shoulder.

'No, as I said, Mary and Dr Silk want to make sure these kids get used to being out and about together before they start mingling with the locals.'

We moved past the city square. 'I thought you were a local, Amy.'

She grinned at me. 'I am. A life-long Loiner since my mother popped me out on the living room floor. I was lying next to my father, who'd fainted when my mother went into labour in the house.'

I scrunched my eyes in confusion. 'What's a Loiner?'

Melissa pushed between us and grabbed my hand, disturbing the bee sitting on her arm. It fluttered its wings and flew past my nose.

'A Loiner is a native to Leeds. My parents dumped me in the woods when I was born, but they left me in York-shire.' She grinned at Amy. 'Which everyone knows is God's country.'

I wasn't sure if she was joking about God and thought better of telling her what I'd heard about the Creator returning to Earth to wipe it clear of living things. So instead, I focused on something we had in common.

'From birth, I've lived in orphanages and care homes, believing my mother had given me up. But only recently, I discovered she'd arranged for my twin sister and me to be taken away from the people who wanted to hurt us.'

Melissa squeezed my hand. 'Do you think that's what might have happened to me?' Her voice rose until it was above the screech of the trains arriving at the station. 'That maybe they did love me after all?'

I gripped her fingers. 'The one thing I've learnt these last few weeks is that anything is possible in this world.' And in all the ones beyond it.

A chilled breath of air settled on my neck and I knew Yuki-Onna was behind me.

'Astomi says his parents gave him away as well.'

We all stopped walking at the same time, standing outside a coffee shop where the customers peered at us through the window.

'What do you mean?' I said.

Yuki-Onna turned to Astomi and they communicated in sign language. Everyone in the coffee shop seemed frozen in time, with cups paused at their lips and cakes half-eaten as they gazed at this strange group of young people. Yuki-Onna appeared to be the centre of attention, with her sparkling green eyes and that snow-white hair hanging over her shoulders, tied into ponytails and reaching to her knees. Even I was spellbound as she spoke.

'Astomi's family brought him to the UK from somewhere in Eastern Europe, he doesn't know where, when he was a baby. They wanted to get his "condition" fixed, and when they couldn't, they left him in a hospital. He was still in a medical facility when he turned sixteen last year. That's when Dr Silk found him and got him released into the care of the Foundation.'

As she spoke, I looked at all of us standing there, transfixed by my reflection in the glass of the shop window. I'd always hated looking at my face, seeing me in a mirror, but now I focused on that pale version of myself and thought of Cassie. And I wondered if all of us were at the Foundation as a result of parents leaving us behind at some point in our lives. Perhaps, like with me, it was for our own good, but with others, it was because their parents had decided they didn't want their unusual children.

Amy grabbed my arm. 'Okay. Let's move this on to the park and away from all these people staring at us.'

I saw what she meant. As well as the gawping coffee shop customers, there were several teenagers on the other side of the road scowling in our direction. Perhaps they were a gang and we were in their territory.

My hand was in Amy's as I pulled her away. 'Come on, then. I'm starving.'

We left as a group, with mutterings about what to order to eat. A couple of minutes later, we were in the park, sprawled on the grass as Amy double-checked what everyone wanted.

'So, I've got two veggie pizzas and one meat feast, two mixed kebabs, a veggie burger, six portions of fries, five cans of Coke and two milkshakes, banana and strawberry. Is that it?'

We all nodded at her as she placed the order into the app on her phone. The milkshakes were for Astomi, who I'd discovered only consumed liquids using a straw pushed up his nose. I was both fascinated and disgusted by the thought of seeing that.

Melissa lay on her back, staring into the marshmallow clouds. A few bees crawled around her in the grass and I carefully avoided them as I sat next to her.

'How long have you had the bees?' I said to her.

She sat up, holding out her hand, which was full of the insects. 'Do you think this is why my parents gave me up?'

'Not if they were like you.'

She hunched her shoulders. 'I suppose it's possible, but I wasn't always like this.'

A bee crawled up my leg and I resisted the urge to flinch. 'What happened?'

'After some kids discovered me in the woods, I was placed into an orphanage, and then fostered. I was a normal girl until my thirteenth birthday, five years ago. That's when the bees appeared and my foster parents panicked. They threw me out of the house and I lived on the streets. That's where the Foundation found me six months ago.'

Amy put the phone into her pocket and joined us. 'The food should be here in thirty minutes.'

An ache surged through my stomach as I spoke to her, and I knew it wasn't because of hunger.

'Are all the kids and teenagers at the Foundation because their parents gave them away?' As well as us, I thought of the others I'd met there, of Sophia, Gregor and Celestine.

Amy shook her head. 'No. Just ask Yuki-Onna.'

All six of us were now sitting in a circle on the grass. We turned to the snow-white hair and shimmering green eyes.

Yuki-Onna smiled. 'My parents came to England from Japan when I was five. They died two years ago, but they loved me unconditionally. I met Amy at the university bar three months ago and she gave me a tour of the Foundation, but she didn't know what I could do until yesterday. She just thought I was cold-blooded.'

There was a flower in her hand, its yellow and red petals trembling as Yuki-Onna waved it towards me. I was about to take it from her when the surrounding air turned icy and we all shivered. Then a soft sheen of ice slipped over the flower until it transformed into a perfect icicle.

'How... how did you do that?' I said.

She shrugged. 'I always could make things cold. My parents did as well. They never saw it as a freakish or a terrible thing, but they knew others would. So they kept their abilities hidden and taught me how to use mine.'

Sandy grabbed the frozen flower from her. 'She's great when we run out of ice.' He licked the flower as if it was a lolly. 'I wish the food would hurry up. My guts are about to eat themselves.' He turned to Melissa. 'Hey, Mel, can you get your bees to whip up some honey to go on this popsicle?'

She laughed and everyone joined in, including me. Was this what it was like to have friends? I suppose it must have been, because being with them meant I hadn't thought of Cassie since we'd left the Foundation building.

I watched them all messing around, complaining half-heartedly about how long the delivery was taking, and wondered if I'd finally found a family to be with. I hardly knew my mother, but now I had plenty of time to change that. And it would be at the same time as I'd be doing what I'd always wanted: to be a scientist working on experiments that would change the world. And I knew they would do that if I could prove human and supernatural development were just two strands of the same evolutionary chain.

But what about Cassie? Could I stay here, with a new family and a career I'd dreamed of, and leave her in America? Even if the video I'd seen was real, who was to say she wasn't forced into doing those things? Yet, wasn't that the life she'd wanted: to kill what she believed were monsters so she could protect the innocent?

The thought of it was about to overwhelm me when the delivery arrived. Amy paid for it using a credit card Dr Silk had given her, and we dived into the food as if none of us had eaten for a week.

For once in my life, I felt normal.

20 CASSIE: REVELATIONS

'How do you get the refugees to the Foundation?' It was the first thing I'd thought about when Vika mentioned it.

Vika picked up the chair I'd thrown to the floor.

'I use various ways, subject to the number travelling and the circumstances. Since the attack on the prime minister, the police have been put on high alert, looking out for anyone who doesn't look "normal." And with the government's State of Emergency, there are military patrols everywhere now.'

'What State of Emergency?' Claudia said.

Vika sighed. 'The British government quickly followed their American counterparts once you and your sister did your thing, Cassie. First, an hour after the death of the American president, they increased the national threat level to CRITICAL. Then they put armed troops on the streets and installed curfews in some places.'

I glanced at Claudia, remembering our time in that underground prison in America. 'So, how do you deal with that when moving people out of the town?'

Vika pushed the chair under the table. 'If it's a large group, say over six, then I have a courier take them in an unmarked van, but I have to ensure I use different couriers every time in case news of the operation leaks out. And trustworthy ones are getting harder to find. The more experienced supernaturals take the train, but it can be a long journey, depending upon the route.'

'And you have a contact there?'

'Yes, the man who runs it, Dr Silk.'

I strode around in circles, my mind a whirling dervish of possibilities. 'So, you'll call him and see if my mother and sister are there?'

I forgot about my so-called father's claims as I focused on a real family reunion.

Then Vika dashed that possibility. 'We don't use human methods of communication; there are far too many risks involved with surveillance.'

I wanted to throw more than the chair now. 'So, what do you do?'

'The only things I trust are ravens.'

'Ravens?' I laughed so hard, I nearly damaged a rib. 'Is this a scene from *Game of Thrones*?'

'I have no idea what that is, but I'll have you know, ravens have been a reliable source of communication for thousands of years. They were here long before digital devices, and they'll be here long after they're gone.' She'd crossed her arms and narrowed her eyes.

'You can't go there, Cassie.' Gabriel stood. 'Your mother isn't to be trusted.'

I was glad he'd got up. Now, I didn't need to throw anything across the room. I grabbed his shirt, lifted him above my head, and bellowed in his face.

'I don't know who you are, but you're not my father. He wouldn't lie about the woman he loved like that.'

Inside me, it was as if a raging, exploding volcano had mixed with a roaring, howling tornado. But, whatever it was, it gave me the strength I'd had before, after drinking angel or demon blood; or from Pandora. I pushed my arm out as far as it would go, lifting the fallen angel high above my head, ready to hurl him into the ceiling thirty feet above.

It was Claudia's hand which stopped me. 'Let him down, Cassie. There are ways to get the truth.'

The anger threatened to overwhelm me, but I felt great. She was right, but I didn't want to let him off that easily. Plus, I thought if I ceased being angry, then my strength would disappear. I kept him there, but spoke to Vika.

'Do you have an address for this Foundation? I can go there and knock on the door.' As long as the authorities didn't haul me in, I'd be okay.

'They're in the phonebook and have a website, so you'll have no trouble finding them.'

That was great news. I wanted to check online, but was reluctant to let Gabriel go. 'Won't you come with me, Vika?'

'I can't. I need to look after the Impossible Palace and those sheltering here.'

Claudia floated in the air to be level with Gabriel. 'You're not going anywhere without me, Cassie Arcane.'

I didn't argue. Then the only thing left to decide was what to do with the broken angel. I dropped him and he hit the floor with a bump.

'Can I use your phone to get internet access out of the Impossible Palace, Vika?'

'Sure.' She handed it to me before helping Gabriel up. 'Have your powers returned, Cassie?'

I tried to fly, and then teleport, but got nothing. 'Nope, it was only adrenalin fuelling me.' Still, it was helpful to know I could increase my strength by channelling my anger. I found the Foundation website and scanned its pages: Dr Julius Silk was listed as its founder and only director, but there was no photo of him. Their mission statement talked about working to help the less unfortunate in society through practical solutions such as providing affordable housing, employment and educational opportunities, and free sources of food and clothing. On top of this, they ran a scientific unit of the organisation, which promised to develop solutions to global problems. There was no description of what those solutions or problems were.

'You can't go there, Cassie. Mary will harm you.'

Gabriel was two feet from me, but my anger had vanished.

'Why should I believe you? You're not even my father.'

'You know that's untrue, Cassie. You said it yourself: blood will find blood. How else did you end up in my cell inside the Devastation? Plus, you can see it in my face; don't deny it.'

How could I? Perhaps my blood in the flower had somehow gone wrong, though I doubted it. But what else he'd said was right: the resemblance to Alice and me was written all over him, especially in those eyes.

'Just because you're my father, it doesn't mean you're telling the truth. Plenty of men, angels or otherwise, lie about those they once loved.'

'There's one way to find out, Cassie: read my mind.'

I shook my head. 'I'm not angry enough for that.'

'Toriyama can do it,' Vika said.

And she was right. I'd known this, but not mentioned it. Why? Was I scared to discover he was speaking the truth and that my mother, the woman I'd sought all my life, only wanted me and Alice for our blood?

Who in their right mind would want to know such a thing?

But I had to. And I never claimed to be in my right mind.

'Do it, then,' I said as I went to the table and drank from the wine bottle. It tasted dry and vile, which was exactly how I felt.

Ten minutes later, I was on my way to getting drunk when the mind-reading monkey returned. Vika explained the situation and Toriyama agreed to do it, but there was one requirement.

'There are some who can tell their lies so compellingly, they convince themselves of the truth of it.' Toriyama stared at Gabriel. 'If this archangel has lived for thousands of years, there's no guarantee they haven't acquired the ability to shadow their true thoughts.'

My legs wobbled a little. 'Great.'

Gabriel was silent as Toriyama climbed onto the table, strode between the empty glasses and took the fallen archangel's fingers. The wine was bitter on my lips and I placed the bottle down before throwing it against the wall. Everyone stared at me as I put my hand up to apologise.

'Perhaps you should leave the room while we do this, Cassie,' Vika said.

I shook my head. 'No. Let's get it over with.' I nodded at Toriyama.

The monkey placed two hands on Gabriel's face. 'When I brought him out of his coma, his mind was nothing but fog and haze, which I brushed away to let his consciousness return to the light. I experienced none of his thoughts or memories then, but now it's different.'

I fought against the urge to leave and listened to the monkey talk. 'There's too much information here and it's overwhelming; so many sights and sounds.' Toriyama's body trembled, their shaking legs a mirror image of mine. 'I see him on the Ark with the Nephilim, hear the orders he had to kill her, but I also feel the love in his heart for this Mary.' The trembling stopped, but the monkey's hairs bristled and stood on end. 'Then the Great Flood arrived and it was terrible.' Huge tears came from Toriyama as their voice dropped to a whisper.

'I see the devastation through his eyes, smell the salt-water as it covers the world, and hear the cries of the doomed. Gabriel can do nothing but watch as he holds Mary's hand while they stand on the deck of the Ark. When the water finally recedes, they flee to the Earth's four corners, constantly hiding from God's agents. But then... then... this is too much.' Toriyama's voice faltered and I could feel their pain. I was jumping up to drag them away when they spoke again. 'Many, many years after the Flood, I see and hear the conversation with Mary. She appears to have no love for what's growing inside her, but has plans for the babies. Gabriel won't have it; he tells her so; and then... then... oh my God.'

Toriyama fell from Gabriel, their body shivering on the table with eyes glazed over. Vika got there before me and took the monkey in her arms.

'He's okay, but I need to get him to a bed and some rest.' She left without another word.

Gabriel had his head in his hands.

'What did Toriyama see at the end?' I said.

My father stared at me as vast shadows crept across his face. He stood, removed his shirt and thrust out his back as if unfurling his great archangel wings, but there was nothing there but broken bone and dying feathers.

Claudia came to me. 'Jesus, who did that to him?'

'The angels when they caught him,' I said.

'No, I lied about that to protect you, Cassie.' He peered at us both. 'Mary did this when she discovered my plans for you and your sister.'

All the light in my heart sank into the abyss. 'My mother mutilated you?' I wouldn't believe it.

'I didn't want you to see what your mother is like. I couldn't bear for you to know what she planned for you and Alice.'

I reached for his shirt and handed it to him. 'You were protecting me again?'

'Every father would have done the same.' He smiled at me. 'She tricked me a few days before your birth, drugged me, mutilated me, and then did something worse.'

'What could be worse than that?' Claudia said. I knew as soon as she spoke.

'My mother stole your Grace.'

He nodded. 'She gorged on demon blood to get the strength she needed, and then, while I was dazed, but awake, Mary thrust her hand into me and removed my Grace.' He turned to us before putting on his shirt and we saw the long scar between his ribs. 'I don't know what she did with it. The next day, she went into labour at the hospital, and the angels caught and imprisoned me. The nurse from the Foundation was already in place in the maternity ward, and she was supposed to take you away and keep you together.'

There was a stunned silence from all three of us as Vika returned.

'I assume you've resolved your family dispute?'

My anger had left me, replaced with a slowly simmering taste of resentment. 'I'm heading to Leeds tomorrow and going straight to this Foundation to see if Alice is there.'

My father slumped into a chair. 'It's no use, Cassie. If your sister is there, your mother will have corrupted her. All you'll be doing is playing into her hands.'

Vika replied to him. 'What will she have done to the refugees I sent to the Foundation?'

He shook his head. 'Nothing good.'

'I'll get the train there and confront her on my own; it's settled.'

Claudia jumped into the air and floated in front of me. 'Like Hell it is. I didn't survive Pandora's furies and travel across the ocean to lose you again.' She held out her arm and I noticed the scars on her wrist. 'Even with Erasmus's help, we had problems getting out of America. I didn't go through all of that to let you leave me again, Cassie.'

I stared at her. 'What happened to you, Claudia?'

'I'll tell you on the journey. You'll need someone to drive, and that's me.' She glanced at Vika. 'Do you have a car I can borrow, something inconspicuous?'

'I'll arrange that. What time do you want to leave?'

I looked at Gabriel. 'When will you be ready, Father?'

He pushed himself from the chair. 'The earlier, the better.'

21 ALICE: MOTHER'S TALK

I fell into my life as a research scientist with ease. By day, the public face of the Foundation worked to improve the lives of the less fortunate in the city. At the same time, inside its underground laboratories, I led a team discovering as much about supernatural biology as we could. At night, I scoured the streets with some of the others. We headed for communities like the one Grace had lived in with the other trolls or sought individual supernaturals who needed our help.

It was the life I'd always dreamed of, working to discover new things that would change the world, and there was no doubt it would do that if we ever made our findings public. Lucy had said governments and other influential organisations were on a path to reveal the truth about the supernatural to humanity. If that was true, I needed to have information to present to the public to show that supernaturals were people just like humans and that they - we, myself - had evolved along similar lines to every other living thing on the planet.

'There's more that connects us than divides us,' Mary told me. 'So let's find those common links.'

It was work that was both satisfying and rewarding, but it had an added benefit as well: working with my mother meant we got to know each other quicker than I thought would happen. Her pride in me, her admiration and love, were evident each time we were together. We rarely talked about Cassie; it was a defence mechanism on my part to hide the guilt and shame I had, whereas, for her I think she found it difficult to worry about someone she'd never known.

There were no more reports from America, no more communications from Dr Silk's contacts. He told us he thought his contacts might have been discovered and dealt with. He never clarified what he meant by that, but it wasn't hard to guess what punishment they'd have suffered.

So, I continued my work for the Foundation, kept getting to know others who were like me, but weren't like me, always hoping we'd find someone who had abilities that could get me to America or deliver a message to Cassie. Of course, she was still at the forefront of my mind, but I surrounded myself with scientific research and night-time quests for the supernatural.

I'd been focusing on my work for the Foundation, collecting blood samples from most of the supernaturals staying there. Then, with Amy's assistance and the team she led, I created a central database of our results. In reality, it was more about distracting me than doing something productive for the Foundation and the community. If I stood still for too long, either physically or emotionally, then all I did was obsess about Cassie.

The first few days after I'd watched that video clip for umpteen times, I'd pestered Mother for more news, but she'd always say Dr Silk was waiting to hear from America. That's when I realised I had to focus on other things, or I'd drive myself mad thinking about what I'd seen.

I'd been patient all my life, with the people and places where I was sent to live, with those who didn't understand me, and with my education. Cassie had survived all that time without me, before our strange first meeting, with at least two years of fighting monsters, so she'd be okay without me again. It was only a few weeks since I'd seen her last. Whatever she was doing in America, she wouldn't need my help; others in the UK needed it more.

That's what I kept telling myself, but at night, when I had to rest, the guilt flooded back like a great deluge. The first few nights were sleepless for me, but after that, I'd sleep like a baby once my head hit the pillow.

It was only when I'd given up all hope of seeing my sister again that the strangest thing happened.

'It's your seventeenth birthday next week, Alice.' My mother pushed the envelope towards me. 'So I think we should start your celebrations early, especially since I've missed all your other birthdays.'

And now Mother had reminded me - unintentionally, I guess - that it was Cassie's birthday next week too. I took the envelope and opened it: it was a Foundation credit card.

'What's this for?'

She caressed my cheek. 'It's about time you had your own financial means of support and, considering the amount of work you've put in here, inside and outside the building, Julius and I believe you should get paid.' She removed her fingers from me and took the card. 'We couldn't open an account in your name, not with the police still looking for you – we must do something about that soon, so thought of this instead. The PIN details are in the envelope and you're limited to £1,000 a month, but it will get you set up.'

I opened my mouth wide enough to swallow a bird. 'You're giving me £1,000 a month?' The most I'd ever had at one time was the £50 a week spending money Artemis provided me before I started university.

'Don't you think you deserve it?'

The card was back in my hand in an instant. 'Oh, definitely.' My mind raced with everything I'd buy, until I realised it was a list of equipment for the lab and science books. I couldn't remember the last time I'd bought something just for the sake of it and not for studying or practical reasons. What did a teenage girl, soon to be seventeen years old, buy herself? I thought about asking Medusa, thinking that even she'd have a better idea than me.

Mother smiled at me. 'I figured you would.'

'I'll go online at lunchtime and see how quickly I can spend the money.'

My mother reached down, got a plastic bag, and put it on the table. 'I think we'll do better than that; it's about time you went proper shopping with your mother. A bit of retail therapy will get your mind off things. I hear there are plenty of exciting shops for teenagers in Leeds.'

My shoulders slumped. 'You know it's a risk for me to go outside in the daylight; you've just said yourself the police are looking for me.'

She dumped the contents of the bag over the table. 'Take it from someone with a few thousand years' experience of how to hide in plain sight: you'll be okay in disguise.' I rifled through the wigs and dark glasses. 'Amy helped me pick these out.' She turned to leave. 'So choose a combination and I'll see you at the front in fifteen minutes.' She pointed at the envelope. 'Memorise the PIN, and then destroy the paper.'

She left before I could reply, not that I had anything to say. I selected a long blonde Marilyn Monroe-type wig and small round John Lennon shades. I was at the entrance five minutes later and waiting for her. Amy was there, scanning through her electronic itinerary for the day.

'Can I help you, Miss?'

I lowered the glasses and winked at her. 'Yes, you can do all my work for today.'

'Jesus, Alice, I didn't recognise you.' I wondered how true that was or whether my mother had put her up to it. 'Where are you going?'

'It's an early birthday shopping trip with my mother.'

'Yes, a little bird told me you'd be seventeen next week.' She leant into me. 'I think there could be cake and a party. Plus, well, I'm not supposed to mention this, but there might be an exceptional person here to croon for you.'

'Like a pop star? I don't listen to music.'

Amy laughed and moved nearer to whisper in my ear.

'No, silly; your mother and Dr Silk have got a siren to sing for you.'

I bumped my wigged head into hers as I jerked up. 'A siren? Don't they lure sailors to their deaths using enchanted music and singing?' That was all I remembered about them from Greek mythology.

She pulled me away from the entrance. 'I know, that's what I thought, but, according to your mother, it was all a - pardon the pun - myth; another set of lies created by men, she said. Anyway, I guess we'll be able to talk to her at some point. I haven't met her yet; she arrived with the recruits last week.'

'My mother found this siren in Leeds? There's a river running through the city, but the sea must be miles away.'

'I think she's part of a group we took in from another town.'

This was news to me. 'The Foundation is bringing in supernaturals from outside Leeds?'

Her eyes glittered with excitement. 'Yes, your mother and Dr Silk are keen to extend our research - well, your research - beyond the city, especially to bring in unique subjects we haven't seen before.'

I glanced around the building. 'I realise this place is big, but how many can we put up here?'

She pushed at her glasses. 'Not all of them stay here, plus I think there are two floors below our laboratories for housing. I've never been down there, so I don't know. I believe there's a special key card for those levels. Dr Silk or Mary would have those.'

My mother strode towards us across the lobby as Amy talked, wearing a short-sleeved knee-length floral dress.

'It's not that warm outside.'

She puckered her lips at me. 'Don't worry, Alice; a week today, you'll be seventeen.' She took my elbow. 'So let's spend some early birthday money.'

WE SPENT HOURS TOGETHER, shopping, having lunch, and seeing the sights. At first, I was concerned someone would see through my flimsy disguise, but we were untroubled during our trip, even though the wig made my head itch the longer the day went on.

Before we returned to the Foundation, she took me for

coffee and cake. I dropped my two full bags at the table and removed my shoes to massage my aching feet.

'How do people do this every weekend?' An old couple in the corner gave me funny looks, which I hoped were to do with me flexing my toes in their direction and not because they recognised I was a wanted fugitive.

'Didn't you enjoy your day out, Alice?'

'Of course, Mother.' I bent my head as the waitress brought our order; she'd barely turned to leave before the chocolate cake was in my mouth. 'But my feet are on fire.' I ate as I spoke. 'I'd rather face another demented angel than go through that ordeal again.' I shivered at the recent memory of fighting through half a dozen young women to get to the changing room in the city's latest trendy fashion shop.

Mother sipped at her tea like a proper English gentlewoman.

'When will you wear the clothes you bought? I especially like the pretty red sleeveless dress.'

It was pretty. 'Don't you think it is too tight and short?' I preferred loose-fitting tops and trousers, not just because they were comfortable, but they were the easiest things to move around in during a fight. But I hadn't fought since the trolls, so maybe that part of my life was over, and if it was, I was unsure if I was happy about it or not.

'Don't be silly, Alice. Most girls your age wear outfits a lot more revealing than that.' As she spoke, two young women a few years older than me walked into the café, wearing painted-on Day-Glo dresses which were a good six inches above their knees. When they sat down, I had to turn away so I didn't see an eyeful.

I finished the rest of the cake. 'I guess so.'

'You must get used to this new world.' She nibbled at a

biscuit. 'It's a lot different from when I was your age, I can tell you.'

The girls opposite gossiped about clothes, nights out and TV shows I knew nothing about. It seemed their world was as different to mine as mine was to what my mother experienced when she was my age. I gazed at her, scrutinising her face and guessing she looked somewhere in her early thirties, yet I knew that wasn't true by a long chalk.

'How old are you, Mother?'

Tea dribbled over her lips as she raised a hand to her mouth. 'My dear child, what a thing to ask someone. Age is only important if you're a cheese.'

I leant closer to her. 'You know what I mean. I know nothing about what your life was like before, well, I saw you at Buckingham Palace. I want to know everything about you and the Nephilim and how you survived all this time.' I waited to get a reaction from her, but she was stony-faced. 'And I want to learn about my father.'

She licked her lips. 'All in good time, Alice.' She bit the biscuit in half and I watched the crumbs tumble onto the pristine tablecloth. 'There is such a lot to tell, but we have to focus on what's important right now, which is the great work you're doing at the Foundation. Julius and I agree it won't be long before we have a breakthrough in understanding the link between supernatural creatures. However, while that is ongoing, you and Amy are making significant strides in finalising a catalogue of the supernatural to analyse the evolution of the species.'

She was correct; there would be plenty of opportunities for discovering her past.

So we finished our cake and returned to the Foundation. And I continued doing all those things she'd said, completing the science, patrolling the city at night, spending time every day together with Mary, doing what a mother and daughter should be doing.

And I stopped worrying about my sister.

Cassie had survived before meeting me and she'd do so again. All she'd wanted was to kill monsters, and, going from that video clip, that's what she was doing.

All I'd ever desired was to be a scientist. Now I was in charge of possibly the greatest scientific study since Darwin, and I was doing it with my mother.

That meant Cassie and I were both happily pursuing our dreams. And fate had brought us together once before, so I was sure it would again if that was the way it was supposed to be.

If only I'd remembered that fate and science don't go together.

22 CASSIE: JOURNEY INTO MYSTERY

We set off early. Vika gave us a mobile phone each, with her number in the Contacts of all three. She'd also placed two sets of dark glasses and wigs in the back of the car: one a disguise for me, the other to keep the sun from Claudia, who wore a pair of thin leather gloves. Gabriel slept behind us while Claudia drove. He was cleaned up and wearing fresh clothes.

Claudia searched through the radio before settling on a station.

I nodded at my father. 'Keep it low. I don't want to wake him up before we get there.'

'Of course, Cassie. He didn't look too good in the Impossible Palace.'

The digital clock on the dashboard ticked over to seven in the morning. 'How long before we arrive?'

She put her seatbelt on. 'I won't rush. There's no need to draw any unwanted attention, so it'll perhaps take about two hours. That leaves plenty of time to park and find the hotel.' Vika had provided us with a credit card and booked accommodation for us before we left.

'I've never been to Leeds.' I peered through the window as we set off. 'Do you know the way?'

'GPS on the phone Vika gave me.' She pointed at it near the steering wheel. 'It's over forty years since I was in England.'

My reflection in the glass unnerved me, so I turned from it and looked at Claudia, peering at her cheekbones and bright eyes.

'I sometimes forget how old you are.'

She laughed as robotic voices on the radio finished singing about computer love.

'You and me both, Cassie.'

I should have tried to get some rest, but there were too many things scrambling inside my head. 'What's it been like, living for so long?' As my seventeenth birthday approached, I couldn't imagine reaching twenty.

Claudia tapped her hand on the steering wheel, but not loudly enough to bother Gabriel in the back. Still, the way he snored, I wasn't sure anything less than a bomb would wake him. That thought sent my fingers to my throat and the spot where the explosives had been not so long ago. I started humming along to a tune about a psycho killer.

'Well, it's had its difficulties, I'll say that.' She glanced at me as we cruised down an empty road. 'But since I met you, it's been all excitement and adventure.'

'You never told me what happened to you in that Section 25 prison.'

'Nothing good ever happens in prison, Cassie.'

'You've been imprisoned before?' I tried not to remember the image of her in chains when I read her mind in America.

'I'm over two hundred years old, my friend. Of course

I've been locked up before, and in a lot worse places than that one.'

She tried to sound upbeat, but I heard the sorrow behind her words. It wasn't my place to have her recount all the suffering she'd endured in her long life, both as a human and a vampire, so I moved the conversation to something else.

'You said you'd tell me how you got those scars after leaving Valhalla.'

Claudia nodded along to the music. 'I did, didn't I.' She put her lips together and whistled for thirty seconds. 'Do you remember the pretty dust devil, Luke?'

I smiled. 'How could I forget him?'

She laughed. 'Yes, you had a little crush on Luke, didn't you?'

Heat rose through me and I scratched along my arm. 'I did not.'

Claudia shook her head. 'Well, anyway, he left us and headed back to his home in New York. That left me and the banshee having to dodge the attention of the Section 25 goons.'

'Colleen? Did she come to England with you?'

'Yes, but only once we'd fought our way to the coast and a boat ride here.'

I remembered the scars on Claudia's wrist. 'Who did you have to fight?'

'When Dr Erasmus arrived to get her brother, Commander Bolt was with her, and he had soldiers with him.' She glanced at me. 'And he wasn't too pleased that most of the troops he'd sent into the supernatural mist with us were dead. If that wasn't enough to infuriate him, discovering all of the Omega Team had disappeared pushed him over the edge. Erasmus helped Luke, Colleen and me slip out of the town, but Bolt must have discovered what she did.'

'So he sent soldiers after you?'

'He did. We nearly made it all the way undetected, but a group of six of them caught up with Colleen and me at the docks. Luke had left us the day before, but I still didn't think we were in any trouble.' Her eyes narrowed. 'You'd expect a vampire and a banshee to handle six soldiers, right?'

'They had weapons that could hurt you,' I said.

'That's correct. How did you know?'

'It was something Vika said about an encounter she recently had in Whitby.' I told her the story of Vika's wound. 'Did the Section 25 soldiers have anything like that?'

Claudia nodded. 'I guess so. They came at us with knives and I laughed at them. That was until one of them cut me on the wrist. I bled immediately and I felt as weak as a baby. Luckily, Colleen dealt with them and we made it to the ship heading to the UK.'

'Do you know how the knife was able to injure you like that?'

She shook her head. 'No. I wanted to take it, but we didn't have the time.'

'What happened to Colleen?'

'I left her in Liverpool. She had things to do in Ireland, while I headed to Whitby.'

We sat silently for a minute. She'd tried to hide it when telling me what had happened to her, but I'd noticed the trembling in her voice. I decided to change the subject as a woman sang about running up a hill.

'Have you had many adventures in England?'

'Ah, now you're talking.' A few other vehicles joined us, mainly lorries heading off to deliver goods up and down the country. 'I was in London at the beginning of 1966, having fled a nasty bunch of vampire hunters in France. Thankfully, a nice gentleman gave me a lift here in his boat; it was my very own Dunkirk. Anyway, it was the height of the swinging sixties in the capital, and I landed at the best time.' She kept her focus on the road as she talked. 'I was strolling down Carnaby Street on a night out, and who should I bump into but George Harrison?'

'Who?'

Her eyes bulged as she scrutinised me. I might have imagined it, but I think there was a slight tremor on her lips. 'You're kidding me. You've never heard of George Harrison?'

'Is he a movie star? I watched a lot of movies when I wasn't hunting monsters.' It felt strange saying that to a teenage vampire. And, of course, she wasn't a teenager.

'Well, he was in a few films with his band, you know, The Beatles.'

'I only know the one who got shot, the hippy guy.'

She sighed heavily. 'I met John, Paul and Ringo through George, and I hung out with them a lot for most of 66. They introduced me to Stevie Wonder, Roy Orbison, the Lovin' Spoonful, the Mamas & the Papas, and Bob Dylan. I spent a long time talking to Stevie Wonder. He was only sixteen then and known as Little Stevie Wonder. We spoke about our heritage and his song writing, so he taught me how to write songs. And then I took that and helped The Beatles that year with a few tunes on *Revolver*. Even you must have heard of *Paperback Writer*?'

A woman with a beautiful voice was singing about pearly dewdrops drops on the radio, whatever they were.

'I don't listen to music much.'

She slapped a free hand on to my knee. 'When this is all over, I'll give you a few lessons in music history.'

'You should write a book about what you've done.'

'I've written a few over the years, never under my name.'

'You didn't want someone tracking you through your vampire life?'

'Oh, people have tried that anyway. No, this was something different.'

'You're shy?'

'Yes, that's it.' She shook her head. 'How many black authors have you heard of, never mind female ones?'

I never got time to read a lot, but I searched my memory and understood what she meant.

'I know of Alice Walker because I've seen *The Color Purple* a few times.'

'Exactly. So I didn't even bother trying to get published under my name. And then, over the decades, I wrote more books, so I used different pseudonyms. It was easier that way.'

'Are any of them famous?'

She winked at me in the mirror. 'A few.'

'We must go to a bookshop when this is over and I'll buy some of yours.' She narrowed her eyes at me. 'Don't worry; it'll be a late-night opening in the winter.'

'That's a promise, but to get that far, we need to have a plan for the Foundation. Do we have one?'

'I'll stride up to the door and ask if my sister or mother is there.'

My father grumbled in the back.

'And what if Gabriel spoke the truth and your mother wants to harm you?'

'That'll never happen.' I had no doubts, regardless of

what my father said and what the monkey had read in his thoughts. Perhaps he had used his archangel abilities to lie about what was on his mind.

Claudia's scowl told me she wasn't convinced about me knocking on the door of the Foundation.

'No, I've got a better plan. They don't know me there. I'll tell them I've come from Whitby looking for somewhere to stay. Then I can have a look around, see what's what, and text you.'

She was correct. It was better than me barging in.

'Okay, there's no argument from me, but you'll have to be careful.'

'Why? I thought you didn't believe what Gabriel said about your mother.'

I glanced at my father sleeping in the back. We'd been driving for more than an hour and I suddenly needed rest. My original intention was to go straight to the Foundation and demand to see my mother. But, since we'd scuppered that for Claudia's more subtle approach, there was no need to rush there. So I could grab a few hours' sleep in the hotel.

'You know what I mean. We don't know what's inside that place. It could be an AEGIS front for all we know. And they might have those weapons that can hurt you.'

She nodded and kept on driving. I had no idea what we were heading into, if it would be another dangerous situation like the one with Saxon and his cult; the thought of seeing Alice and my mother again was the only thing keeping me going.

I settled into the seat and focused on the music, leaving Claudia to drive without me distracting her. The time appeared to disappear in a haze as someone sang about being alone in bedsit land on the radio. Then she tapped me on the knee.

'We've got a problem.'

She pointed to the mirror and I saw what she meant: flashing lights were coming towards us.

'There might have been an accident up ahead,' I said. 'It could be an ambulance.'

'Let's hope so.' Claudia decreased her speed. The GPS screen showed us at twenty-five minutes from Leeds as the lights got closer. I peered at the police car parallel to us.

'Crap!' I said.

Claudia gripped the steering wheel. 'We can try to outrun them.'

I glanced out of the window at the number of vehicles on the road, picturing the carnage we'd cause if she attempted to speed away. We couldn't take that risk. And maybe it was completely innocent.

'No,' I said. 'There's a lay-by coming up.' I looked over at the policewoman pointing at the spot I'd seen. 'Let's pull over and see what they want.'

Claudia grunted and did what I'd said. 'It's broad daylight outside, Cassie. I haven't fed today, so I can't get out of the car without the sun burning the flesh from me, even with the hat and dark glasses for protection.'

'It's okay, I'll speak to them. I'll say we're sisters and we borrowed the car from our mother. They can have Vika's phone number to call her to confirm.'

Claudia removed her seatbelt. 'I love your confidence, my friend, but we should have a backup plan as well.'

In the mirror, I watched two police officers step out of their car and approach ours.

'What do you suggest?'

She turned to me. 'Remember when you told me it was Pandora's blood which helped you defeat her, and to escape from those angels?' I nodded. 'Well, I may not be an ancient deity, but if you drink some of my blood, it might resurrect your Arcane abilities so you can teleport the three of us out of here.'

I shook my head and glanced into the back at the sleeping angel.

'I'm not drinking your blood. What shall we say about Gabriel?'

'Tell them he's our old man and he's having a kip. So it's not a total lie.'

As I thought about that, the female copper knocked on Claudia's window. She wound it down to speak to her.

'Was I going too fast, Officer?'

'Can you step out of the car, please?' Her face was unmoving with a voice less emotional than a speaking clock.

Claudia turned to me and whispered, 'We're screwed.'

I didn't know what to do. Then Gabriel woke up.

'What's going on here? I know my rights. We don't live in a police state yet, you know.'

His tone was full of bravado and bluster as he winked at me. Then he got out of the car to speak to the coppers.

Claudia leant into me. 'If he distracts them, we might be able to get far enough away to lose them.'

'I'm not leaving him here.' I hadn't rescued him from the Devastation and war in Heaven to leave him by the side of the road outside Garforth.

She bit her finger and pushed it towards me. 'Then drink this so you can do your stuff to get the three of us away from these cops.'

I grimaced at her, watching as the red trickled down her skin. I'd tasted the blood of others, so what difference did it make to take hers now? I was about to decide when I saw my father collapse to the ground outside.

'What happened?' I leapt out of the car and ran to him.

My knees creaked as I bent to get hold of his head. Cars and trucks were speeding by only a few feet away, sending exhaust fumes at me. I coughed loudly as I got one hand under his neck and turned Gabriel towards me. Smoke was clinging to my eyes as I tried to wipe it away and make sense of what I was seeing: there was a plastic dart in my father's throat.

A volcano erupted through my veins as I jerked my head towards the female copper.

That's when she hit me in the face with something hard.

The force of it knocked me backwards and onto the grass verge on the road. Dirt and smoke jumped between my lips as I struggled to breathe. I pulled at my chest as I tried to stand, only to find the boot of the male copper planted into my ribs.

'Stay down and you won't get hurt, kid.'

His weight pressed on me as I glanced at the car, searching for what had happened to Claudia. If the female police officer dragged her out, then neither the hat nor the glasses could protect her from the sun for long.

I should have taken that blood.

'What do you want?' The words crawled out of my mouth.

He picked at his teeth as he grinned at me. 'You're a wanted fugitive, kid, you and the other two.'

'You can't do this to us. There are laws in this country.'

He laughed at me. 'That's all gone now, girl. We live in different times. Britain is under attack. This is the State of Emergency, and we can do whatever we want to scum like you. Hell, the whole civilised world is at war with you commie bastards.'

The woman joined him as he ranted at me. 'It's not the

communists, you idiot.' She towered over me. 'It's the monsters we're fighting, so stop wasting your time with this girl.'

Before I could say anything, she hit me in the head with something as hard as a stone.

Before the lights went out, the last thing I saw was the two of them dragging Claudia from the car.

23 ALICE: NOISE ANNOYS

'The night my parents died, I had a vision of the end of the world.'

Yuki-Onna was sitting next to me while Amy and I catalogued the newest recruits to the Foundation: a group of six who'd arrived overnight. Melissa and the others were upstairs, playing computer games or watching TV. Dr Silk had created several training courses during my mother's imprisonment in Hell, but every once in a while, Foundation residents were allowed a little relaxation. All except me, and that was my choice. I didn't feel I deserved to relax while Cassie and I were still separated. I had my work and that was enough to keep me occupied.

I looked at Yuki-Onna. 'Are you one of those who can see the future?'

She ran her finger around a test tube on the table and it turned to ice. 'No, but I think it might have been a premonition of what was to happen to them.'

I peered into her green eyes and assumed she wanted to talk about that night.

'Was it an accident?'

She nodded. 'That's what the police told me. Their car went off a bridge and into a river.' She moved closer to me. 'The strange thing is, well, the police never found their bodies, but they did recover the car.'

'A river's current can be fierce at times, dragging people away in an instant.'

'Yes, I understand that, but I would have expected one of them to freeze the surrounding water, just enough to swim to the top of it.'

'Perhaps they were unconscious.'

Yuki-Onna was considering my words when my mother and Dr Silk entered the workshop. She whispered something to him before heading to me.

'Have you got time for a break, Daughter?'

I pushed the laptop away from the screen displaying the latest bloodwork we'd gathered from a sylph, an air spirit named Julia. She was floating around the laboratory, talking to Sophia the sprite. Julia didn't have wings like Sophia, but I wondered if there was a DNA connection between the two species. I was keen to work on it and compare their blood, but now that my mother and Silk had arrived, it would have to wait. I'd learned while working with my mother how impatient she'd get if she couldn't get her way.

Only yesterday, I'd seen her scream at Silk when one of their experiments had gone wrong. Neither of them knew I was outside the room and I kept it like that as I left.

'Of course, Mother, but today isn't a shopping trip, is it?' Maybe I'd forgotten and she was mad at me. But she didn't look upset.

'No, it's not that, Alice. Julius and I thought it was time you saw the rest of the facility; there's other work going on as well as yours, which you should be aware of.'

My eyes widened when she said that. It would be interesting to observe what others were doing in the Foundation. I nodded to Yuki-Onna, promising myself I'd talk to her again about her parents. It was all well and good working through blood and DNA samples, but I had to remember that some of these people were my friends and not just guinea pigs in a lab.

I left the slides with Amy and followed Mother to the lift. As far as I knew, we were already on the lowest accessible level, but she pressed her finger into the number plate and we descended.

'The supernatural database is growing every day,' I said as we headed down. 'Not all the subjects are from Leeds, though, are they?'

As usual, Silk was silent as if he was nervous about talking to me, but she nodded. 'We get a few coming over from nearby towns and cities.' Her eyes glittered with pleasure. 'We're becoming known in the supernatural community now.'

I found it strange to think of a supernatural community. 'Aren't you worried the authorities might find out, people like AEGIS?' The government had lessened the terrorist threat level to the country, but I still felt uncomfortable every time I left the building.

She shook her head. 'We'll be fine, Alice. There's nothing to worry about from them, the police, or the British government. There are others we should be more concerned with.' She didn't elaborate as the lift opened and we walked into a laboratory I hadn't seen before.

There was a ringing in my ears and I rubbed my fingers against the side of my head. 'Are you testing low-level sonic equipment in here?' It wasn't painful, more like an itch in the centre of the ear which I couldn't reach.

My mother placed her hand on my arm. 'Do you have a headache, Alice?'

I put on my best smile. 'No, I'm fine, but there's a humming sound in the middle of my skull. Don't you two hear it?'

They both shook their heads. My mother went to a locked cupboard and punched in a four-digit password.

'It might have something to do with this.' She removed a long glass container and placed it on the table near us. I stared at the contents with amazement.

'Where did you find this?' I put my hands on the glass and the buzzing in my head increased, but not painfully; this time, it was more like a favourite lullaby whispered to me.

'One of our operatives discovered it on a train. Do you know what it is?'

'It's the Blade of Reality.' Something Cassie and I had lost at Newcastle train station weeks ago. But now I'd found it again.

Dr Silk filmed everything on his phone. 'And what exactly is the Blade of Reality?'

'It's a method of travelling from one place to another, anywhere, instantaneously.'

My mother put her hand on mine on top of the glass. 'And how does it do that?'

'I'm not sure about the mechanics of it, but Kai - our friend who lent it to Cassie and me - said you have to use it to cut into the air while picturing where you want to go. You need to have an image of the place you're travelling to for it to work. Then you slice through space, creating a door or a window to step through.'

My mother removed her hands from the glass and

opened the case. She reached in to get the Blade, picking it up gently, and then handed it to me.

'Why don't you show us how it works?'

I took the handle and the air sang inside my head. 'I've never used it before; it was Cassie who did.'

'But I'm sure you know how.'

'I'll try.' I gripped it in my hand, wondering what the proper name was for a small sword; it was bigger than a dagger, but still light. 'Where do you want to go?'

My mother looked at Silk. 'Hawaii would be nice this time of the year, wouldn't it, Julius?' They both laughed at a joke I didn't get.

'I don't know what that looks like.'

'If Julius showed you a photo on his phone, would that work?'

'I think so, as long as it's an actual place. Kai said the Blade couldn't cut into imaginary locations.'

Dr Silk found what he wanted and placed the mobile to my face. It showed a beautiful sandy beach leading down to a sparkling azure sea. 'Will this do?'

'I'll try.' I took two steps back from my mother and Dr Silk, wary I might stumble and hurt one of them. Then I held my arm out and remembered how Kai and Cassie had used the Blade before. I started in the top left, level with my head, and cut a wide length across, then brought it down and followed all the way around into the shape of a door. Nothing had changed and they both looked disappointed.

'Nothing's happened, Alice,' my mother said.

I bent to where the bottom line wavered in the air. 'Watch this.' I found the corner edge, and then peeled reality away until it flipped open like a book cover. The sea breeze drifted through the gap before we gazed into it.

Dr Silk put a hand to his chin. 'Oh, my goodness.'

She slapped him on the back. 'Indeed, so go and try it, Julius.'

He hesitated for a second before moving towards it and stepping through; he disappeared from view.

'Are you okay?' I said.

'I'm great.' His voice floated to us from the other side of the world.

My mother slipped next to me. 'Can we close it up and leave him there?'

I looked at her, unsure if she was joking or not. 'I can. Is that what you want?'

Before she replied, he stepped through and returned. 'It's amazing, Mary. You should try it.'

She grinned. 'Perhaps I will, but somewhere nicer than Hawaii next time.' She took the Blade from me while I closed the gap by dragging the reality skin I'd created back to where I'd sliced it. The section sucked into the hole like air leaking from a balloon.

Silk had a seashell in his fingers and dropped sand to the floor. 'What a wonderful thing it is.'

My mother placed the Blade on the table next to the glass container.

'Do you know what's inside the Blade, Alice?'

I screwed up my eyes. 'Inside? Isn't it solid steel?'

'That's what we thought until we put it through an x-ray.' She opened a drawer in the table and removed a thin scalpel, which she used to prise the Blade apart, taking away one side of the metal. My legs buckled when I saw what was inside it.

'That's organic material.'

She didn't hide her excitement. 'Yes: blood, bones, sinew, and organs we've never seen before.' My mother gazed at me. 'Do you hear it speaking to you?'

I nodded. 'What is it?'

'I can hear it just a little, but Julius can't hear anything. I believe it's telepathic, which is how it picks up the image in your mind of where you want to go, and then when you cut a shape with the Blade, it opens up a portal using tele-portation.'

I needed to sit down. 'This is fascinating.'

My mother put the Blade back together again. 'I know.' She let Julius return it to the case and held my arm. 'Can you see how much more there is for us to discover about the supernatural?' She took me to the other side of the room.

'It's marvellous.' My mind raced with all the scientific discoveries I'd make, and then present to the world as the new theory of evolution on this planet. As I considered that, Silk's phone made a huge vibrating noise. I watched him stare at his screen for two minutes and all the colour drain from his face.

'You need to see this, Mary.'

I left them to it and went to the case containing the Blade. All that time, we'd had it and hadn't realised it was a living thing. Had Kai known?

'Alice, can you come here?' It sounded more like a command than a request from my mother, so I did as she said. Then she handed me Silk's phone. 'You need to watch this.'

She pressed play on the video before I could respond. There was no sound, only the sight of about a dozen people kneeling in a derelict building. The camera zoomed into them and I guessed they were in Asia. Then a young woman stepped into view, brandishing a scythe. I didn't gasp when I recognised Cassie; somehow, I knew this would be about her. I forced myself to continue watching, never taking my focus from her. When she'd finished, a man came in and gathered all the heads. He wore a uniform with a small American flag on the arm and the number twenty-five underneath it. He stared into the lens and I'd swear I'd seen him before.

'That can't be Cassie.'

My mother sighed. 'I'm not going to argue about it, Alice; you must make up your mind. But Julius's contacts say she's working for this US organisation now, Section 25. They're killing humans and the supernatural without discrimination. And they're coming here to stop our work.'

'Why would they do that?'

My mother touched my arm. 'They want to keep our discoveries secret. That way, it's easier for them to justify hunting and killing supernaturals.'

'Who was the man helping her?'

She returned the phone to Silk. 'That's no man, Alice. He's your father.'

I found a chair and slumped into it. In the back of my head, the Blade sang to me.

I sat there wondering what I'd do when I saw my sister again.

Then I blacked out.

24 CASSIE: LOVE LIKE BLOOD

A thousand dancing penguins were having a good time inside my head when I woke. I rubbed at the bruise on the back of my neck and scanned the surroundings: it was a large building, a derelict warehouse by the look of it. The rafters were fifty feet above me, hanging below a cluster of broken windows and home to dozens of pigeons that appeared to have crapped on the floor long before I got there.

I stood as the ache spread through my bones and into my legs. The two coppers weren't there, but neither were Claudia or my father.

Were they still alive?

There was a dirty leather sofa in the middle of the room and I staggered towards it. If the police had brought me here, then surely the others were as well; there had been no need to kill them.

Unless Claudia had fought back as they'd got her out of the car.

That was the last thing I remembered: her dragged into the road.

Shit, shit, shit!

I smacked my fist into the sofa and screamed a shriek loud enough to scatter the birds above me.

And to bring someone else into the room.

'You're finally awake.'

I scratched at my ears in the knowledge I recognised that voice. But it was impossible. The last time I'd seen him was deep underground in a secret prison in America.

Yet, when I turned, there he was: the man who'd sent me and others into a town covered by a supernatural cloud to rescue the president of the United States. Commander Bolt of Section 25, the clandestine American organisation tasked to track down and capture supernatural beings.

I tensed my legs, ready to rush him until he pointed above me and I looked up to see what I'd missed earlier.

'Cameras?'

Bolt nodded. 'One false move from you and the vampire and the old bloke you were with will be killed.'

I grasped at my chest. 'Claudia's alive?'

'For now.' The light sneaked into the building through the broken glass. 'Where I'm from, the sunsets are a beautiful mixture of orange and pink. People come from all over to see them, unaware that the pollution creates such a sight.' He smiled at me. 'Even the prettiest stars are born from death.'

They had to be keeping Claudia and Gabriel somewhere close by. So I just had to keep him talking until I could find them and get all three of us out of there.

'I'm honoured, Bolt, that you travelled all the way from America to see me.'

His laugh made my spine itch. 'Don't be stupid, kid. I know you didn't do anything in Valhalla. That Irish bitch told me she and the others saved President Dixon while you ran away like a scared little girl. I didn't come here for you.'

'So why did those coppers attack me?'

He continued to pick at his teeth as he talked. 'I'm in the UK as a special liaison from Section 25 with our British counterparts, AEGIS. I just got lucky to be here when one of the patrols pulled you and the others over.' He moved close enough to me, I could gouge his eyes out before anyone could rush in to help him.

But I didn't. 'Luck more than skill seems to be you to a tee, Bolt.'

'You might be right, kid. So do you want to tell me who the guy is we found in the car with you and the vampire?'

It was my turn to laugh. 'You'll get nothing from me.'

He shook his head. 'That's a shame. I always like to get to know a man before he dies.'

I dug my nails into my palms. 'What?'

'Would you like to see your friends?' Before I could reply, he'd turned his back on me and walked to the door at the end of the room. I followed him through and held my breath. He grinned at me. 'I'll say one thing for the Brits: they're far more ruthless than us when dealing with monsters.'

Bolt moved away, leaving me to stare at the nightmare surrounding me. Whereas the other room was sparse and old, this place was modern and full of people: dozens of them dressed in white coats resembling doctors or scientists, buzzing around like bees between the medical equipment and computer screens.

'What is this?' I said.

Bolt beamed at me. 'Impressive, isn't it? I bet even Dr Erasmus would love something as good as this to slice and dice her way through our collection of monsters.'

Most of the trolleys were empty, but at least half a dozen had people strapped to them; no, not people: supernatural creatures. I didn't recognise any of them apart from the two at the end: Claudia and Gabriel.

My heart told me to rush to them, to help them, but my brain urged caution. There were armed soldiers everywhere, standing at every exit, at least ten of them. Even with my full power, I'd struggle to overpower the forces in the room.

And right now, I had no Arcane abilities. All I had was my own strength, which wasn't much.

But I had to do something.

I glared at Bolt. 'What are you going to do with them?'

'Don't worry, kid. You'll have the best view when we cut your vamp friend open.' He waved at a white-uniformed man to approach Claudia. 'But, before we begin, why don't you tell me who the old guy is?' I didn't respond, spending all my energy controlling my anger. 'Okay, be like that. But the doctors did find the remains of his wings. Is he some type of birdman? Is that it?' He kept on grinning at me. 'I hope so. His DNA will add something new to all the others we have.'

I couldn't remove my eyes from the scalpel in the hand of the man next to Claudia.

'You're cutting people open to experiment on them and take their DNA?'

Bolt's laughter was like a howl. 'They're not people, you stupid girl. They're monsters just like you. And they're terrorists, so they'll be treated as such.'

My father lay constrained on a trolley next to Claudia, with nothing but the thickness of a blade between them. I watched as he tried to reach for her as the doctor cut into Claudia's chest.

Her agonised howl reached my ears before anyone else and I dropped to my knees in pain. I put my face in my hands only for a second before removing them and scanning the room again. What chance did I have in saving us all?

Only one.

I stood and spoke to Bolt.

'If you let me say goodbye to Claudia, I'll tell you about the man you found with us.'

He shook his head. 'He's a birdman, that's all. But, fascinating as that seems, and some of the doctors are quite keen to see if they can replicate his wings on our human guinea pigs, I'm not going to give you anything, girl.'

'Gabriel is an angel,' I said.

The doctor stopped cutting into Claudia as Bolt stood there with his mouth catching flies.

'There are no such things as angels,' Bolt said.

I smiled at him. 'How sweet and reasonable the pale shadows of those who smile from some dim corner of their mind.'

'What?' he said.

'The supernatural world is so much bigger than you realise, Bolt. Angels and demons exist, as do the Devil and God the Creator. I've visited Heaven and Hell and survived Limbo and Purgatory. I could tell you about all of these things so you could pass them on to your superiors in Section 25. Just think how famous and influential that would make you.'

He stumbled towards me. 'Yes, tell me everything now.'

I held up my hand. 'I will, I promise, but I need to say goodbye to Claudia first.'

Bolt stood there, looking as if the hamster in his head was going mad in its little wheel. If he'd thought about it, he might have wondered why I'd never asked for him to spare Claudia's life.

'Make it quick,' he said.

So I did. I ran to Claudia and pushed the doctor out of the way. Her chest was open from her neck down to her navel. I tried not to look at her guts spilling out and took her hand. There was blood on her mouth as she smiled at me. Then I reached over and held my father's fingers.

Then I dipped forward and kissed Claudia on the lips. Her blood was sweet and tasted of honey. I drank as much as I could before I turned to Bolt.

'The next time I see you, I'll kill you.'

Then Claudia's blood dripped into my stomach and raced through my cells.

And I teleported us out of there.

We landed in a heap in a field in Leeds. Across the road was the hotel Vika had booked for us before we left Whitby, looking precisely as I'd seen it in the photo on the website.

Claudia groaned and I leant over her, unsure of what to do about her wounds. At least it was early evening.

'What do I do?' I said.

Gabriel bent to kneel next to me. 'She'll be fine. She just needs time to heal.'

Claudia put her hands over her stomach and grimaced. 'That's easy for you to say.'

I scanned the area. 'We can't stay here. Someone will see us and come over.'

My father removed his jacket and handed it to me. 'Put this around her and make sure her guts don't fall out.'

'What are you going to do?'

He undid the top button on his shirt. 'I'll check into the hotel. Then I'll come and get you two.' He peered at Claudia. 'She should have healed in a few hours. We'll rest and recuperate in the room while she does.'

Before I could reply, he was off and across the road.

I sighed and spoke to Claudia.

'Can you get up without spilling your organs everywhere?'

She grimaced. 'I suppose so. Luckily that doctor didn't cut too deep into me.'

Claudia sat up a little, keeping hold of her stomach, while I got her into Gabriel's jacket and buttoned it up.

I held on to her and hoped for the best. Then I remembered how we'd escaped. The taste of Claudia's blood had left me and I knew I was only an average teenager again.

'Bolt's a dead man the next time I see him.'

'Not if I get to him first.' She laughed through gritted teeth.

I smiled at her. 'Are you bothered I drank your blood to get us out of there?'

She pushed her shoulder into mine. 'Of course not. It was my idea, remember. And anyway, it's not like it means we're engaged or anything.'

I couldn't stop laughing as my father returned.

'What's so funny?' he said.

Claudia grinned at him. 'Cassie thinks I look better in this jacket than you do, even with my guts hanging out of me.'

Gabriel looked at me. 'Is she okay to get into the hotel without spilling bits everywhere?'

'We'll soon find out.'

I helped Claudia up. Gabriel took one side, with me on the other. Then we guided her across the road and into the building. Nobody batted an eyelid as my father led us into the lift and we went upstairs. We got her into the room and closed all the curtains.

'Put me in the shower,' she said.

'What?' I replied.

'Because it will be easier to clean up the blood while she heals,' Gabriel said.

We helped her into the shower and got her as comfortable as we could.

'How long will this take?' I said.

My father rolled up his sleeve and offered Claudia his wrist. 'This will help.'

Before I could protest, she bit into his flesh and drank.

I sat against the wall in the bathroom and watched her feed on his blood.

After two minutes, he pushed her off him and stood, his legs shaking as he stumbled into the other room. I moved to Claudia to see if she was okay, noticing that her wounds were already healing.

She licked the blood from her fingers. 'It shouldn't be long now.'

I left her and went to check on him. He lay on the bed with a towel wrapped around his wrist.

He coughed violently as he smiled at me. 'A couple of hours' rest for us all and we should be good to go.'

I squeezed his hand and left him to sleep, retiring to the other bed in the corner. The hotel was close to the Foundation, and I had to resist the temptation to go to the window and peek from behind the curtains to see where I hoped my sister and mother were.

'He's worse than you know, Cassie.'

I looked up to see Claudia, her top covered in blood, but healed.

'I know. The loss of his wings and his Grace is killing

him.' I was beginning to believe that being with me and the thought of seeing Alice were the only things keeping him going.

'Me drinking his blood won't have helped.'

'We had no choice. He knew that.'

'Maybe we should get him to a hospital.'

'And tell them what?' I didn't want to see him like this either, but I didn't know what our options were. 'How would we explain the mutilated wings and burnt feathers on his back?'

'He's not an archangel anymore, Cassie; he's just a lost Heavenly Host in human form. There's no going back for him, no matter what happens here. Perhaps human doctors can help him.'

'I wish that were true, Claudia, but even if it was, do you think he'd sit in a hospital while we deal with the Foundation? He'd leave there as soon as we were out of the door and head straight for my mother.' I couldn't see any other way this would work. 'We have to keep him with us, at least until you get inside and report what you find.'

There was no more discussion after that. I drifted in and out of sleep for two hours while she listened to music on headphones. Then she left and I watched Gabriel slumber.

I wanted to ask him questions about his life, about Mary, about how much he'd missed Alice and me. But I didn't. Instead, I sat there in silence and watched the sun finally disappear.

Then Claudia texted me.

My eyes fluttered open as someone hammered nails into the back of my head. The smell of burnt copper made my nose twitch. It was only when I went to scratch it that I realised I was strapped to a chair.

'You look exactly like your sister.' The unknown voice was next to me. 'But she's got better ears.'

I twisted my neck to see her, flexing my arms and legs to break my bonds, but I didn't have the strength. She was tied up as well. 'You Brits know how to show a Yank a good time.'

She was African-American and looked about my age.

'What happened?'

'I don't know about you, Alice, but someone shot me so full of vampire deterrent, I think there's a herd of pygmy elephants partying inside my skull.' She tried to grin. 'My name's Claudia, I'm Cassie's friend.'

'No more talking, vamp.' It was Dr Silk's voice behind me. Then he and Mary came around to face us.

I glared at her. 'What's going on, Mother?'

Silk went into the corner and wheeled over a large

covered trolley. Then he got another one, which contained the Blade of Reality in a glass cabinet. It was humming inside my head, just below the pain of the nails thumping into my brain. That humming was the last thing I remembered before waking up like this. Had the Blade damaged me somehow?

'I'm sorry, Alice, but the restraints are for your own good. Your sister and father are heading here, and I had to make sure you responded the right way, for everyone's safety.'

'Cassie is coming here? With my father?' I struggled against the straps, pushing with all my strength, as my heart beat against my ribs.

My mother slammed her hand on to the trolley and the glass containing the Blade of Reality shook. 'Didn't I just say that? Weren't you listening?' She turned to Silk. 'I told you she could be as dumb as she is brilliant.'

It was the anger I'd glimpsed from her before. 'What do you think I'll do when Cassie arrives?' I strained again, with the same results.

'We can't trust her, Alice. You know this because of the videos of her working with the American military group, Section 25. I'd hoped, after seeing what she's doing for them, you'd realise she's not on our side. But even with everything you've witnessed of her killing innocents, I couldn't guarantee you wouldn't help her destroy all our work here.'

I shook my head and bit into my top lip. 'Why would Cassie do that? She doesn't know about this place. And even if she did, we're not in a war zone.'

She moved towards me. 'It's your father's influence, Alice. He's corrupted her mind, got her working for the Americans, and now he's desperate to stop me from defending myself again.' Her anger had disappeared. She came over and put a hand on my face. 'He wants to prevent me from protecting you and the world.'

'Who are you protecting me from, Mother?'

'I told you before. God and all Their followers, both human and angel, will soon cleanse the planet so They can erase the Nephilim and the Arcane from existence. Don't forget the Creator sent your father to murder me. After all this time, he hasn't forgotten that mission.'

'You said he loved you, that he betrayed God to save you.'

My mother wiped a tear from her eye. 'Yes, he did. But he wanted me for himself, Alice. As soon as he discovered my pregnancy, he changed. He was going to kill you while you were still inside me. And he would have if I hadn't escaped and arranged for you and your sister to be taken from the hospital and hidden from him and all the others who searched for you. Now, with the help of Section 25, he's twisted your sister's mind to think as he does. Cassie is just an unthinking killing machine now, as we saw in those clips.'

'That's a bunch of baloney. We came here to save Alice from you. Cassie loves her sister. I don't know what videos you're talking about, but she hasn't killed anyone, supernatural or human.' The American girl, Claudia, bounced up and down in her chair. 'This stuff you pumped into me will wear off eventually, and then I'll get you two to tell the truth before I rip your throats out.'

'Ignore the vampire, Alice; she doesn't know what she's talking about.' My mother placed one hand on the covered trolley. 'And she came here to spy on us and to sabotage our work.'

Steam flew from my ears. 'There's nothing to sabotage,

Mother.' I nearly spat at her as I pulled at my bonds. 'And I'm having a hard time believing you since you strapped me to this chair. So cut me free and I promise to listen to you.'

'It's too late for that, Alice.' She pulled away the cover like a magician at a show, but there were no cuddly rabbits or cute assistants on display.

'What the...?' Claudia said as she stopped banging her seat on the floor.

'Beauty is in the eye of the beholder, they say, but I don't think any mother could love these things.' She looked straight at me. 'Do you, Alice?'

I didn't reply, with my gaze focused on the deformed foetuses and babies inside four jars on the trolley. Their heads and bodies were all twisted and tortured, with faces pressed against the glass. They stared at me through distorted eyes.

But they were dead.

'What have you done, Mother?' Sickness rushed up to my throat and I had to stop myself from throwing up.

'Say hello to your half-brothers and sisters, Alice. They're slightly older than you, but not nearly as useful.' She glanced at Silk. 'I'm surprised Julius kept them all this time, but I'm glad he did; it's a timely reminder of my failures.'

Silk returned the cover over the top of the deformed infants and I was thankful for it. 'I couldn't dispose of any part of you, Mary, especially when they took you from me.'

He wheeled the trolley back into the shadows as the pain in my head increased a thousand fold.

'You've been lying to me all this time.'

'No, Alice. I told you the truth. I have to defend myself. I won't be hunted anymore. I begged your father to help me, but he refused.' She glanced into the corner where Silk was dragging out another trolley. 'Luckily, Julius stepped in to aid me with my work. But the Morningstar abducted me, and then sold me like chattel to that pathetic vampire.'

'Dracula said he loved you.'

Her laugh cut through me like a knife. 'Yes, and that was his undoing. But, whether human or celestial, love is always the downfall. The sooner you learn that lesson, the better it will be for you, my daughter.'

'What are those things in the jars?'

She let out a huge sigh. 'Those are my early experiments, the ones your father discovered, but it was too late by then since I was already pregnant.'

'What were they experiments for?'

'I swore I wouldn't hide anymore, but Gabriel said we had no choice. God's agents were everywhere, and when the Creator returned, there would be no more hiding places for me. "So what's the point of running" I asked him. "We have to fight back." He laughed at me and wanted to know how we could do that, for how could any living creature defeat the Creator? But then I got to thinking about the Great Flood sent to destroy the Nephilim.'

She pulled over a chair and sat opposite me. Claudia stared at her. 'Don't you think that was an overreaction? There can't have been more than thirty of us on the planet, yet the All-Knowing, All-Powerful engulfed the world in water just to kill us. It made little sense at all.'

'Unless God is bonkers,' Claudia said.

My mother nodded. 'That's probably true, but as the years went by and Gabriel and I moved from one hiding place to the next, I wondered if there wasn't more to it.'

The humming inside my head continued to grow. 'Such as?'

'Well, I said it was an overreaction, but the more I

thought about it, I believed God sent the Great Flood because They were scared.'

'Scared of what, Mother? You?'

'God was fearful of what I could create. I am the last of the Nephilim, birthed from the union of archangel and human, and you, Alice, and your sister are the Arcane, birthed from Nephilim and archangel. Your blood is unique, and inside it is the potential to be greater than God. That's what the Creator foresaw and it terrified Them. So They're coming back to kill you and your sister, Alice, and every other living thing is collateral damage. The only way to stop Them is to create our army; to create my army.'

I shook my head. 'It's nonsense, Mother. It can't be done.'

'But there's a precedent, Daughter. And you've met them.'

I wanted to dunk my face underwater to prevent it from exploding. 'What?'

'Demons, Alice; where do you think they came from?'

I dredged the back of my thumping brain to recall what I'd heard. 'They're something to do with Lucy.'

'Yes, the First of the Fallen needed an army for their war against God and the Heavenly Host. The angels that followed Lucy from Heaven weren't enough, so they needed something else.' She glanced over to where Silk was pulling at another trolley in the shadows. 'And just like me, they had their early failures, but they got it right, eventually.'

'What do you mean by failures?'

'Where do supernatural creatures come from? Satan wouldn't use human blood because their hate for the Creator's favourites was too strong, so they turned to the animal kingdom.'

'You're lying.'

'What do you think a mixture of Satan's blood and a wolf would produce?'

That seemed too obvious 'A werewolf?'

'Exactly, and with a bat, you get a vampire; with a cat, the result is a witch, and so on.'

'I don't believe it. We were told supernatural creatures, so-called celestials, are God's creations.'

'Myths and legends, stories and folk tales, fake news and post-truth. Why do you think the Greeks believed Zeus produced unusual offspring from - how shall I put this? - close friendships with certain animals?'

My heart crawled up my throat. 'Is this what you want for Cassie and me?'

My mother grinned and shook her head. 'No, there'll be none of that for my sweet daughters; no coupling with anybody. I knew it was more about manipulating your blood, which is what I've been doing the last few weeks, thanks to your unknowing help.'

'You've been taking my blood?'

'A little drug at night for sleep and you never felt a thing.' She nodded towards the shadows. 'And now we have success.'

Silk wheeled over a trolley and there was no revelation this time: these four jars contained living breathing babies at various stages of development. The first looked about a week old, the last about six months.

'How did you do this, Mother?'

'The accelerated growth is a surprise, but perfect for what I need.' Her smile unnerved me. 'I call them the Alisium; what do you think?'

I turned my head to the side and threw up. Silk came

over and wiped my mouth clean, his cold hands creeping over my flesh. I stopped myself from puking again.

'What did you mix my blood with?'

'Now, now, Daughter; a good geneticist never gives away their secrets. If you promise to work with me, then I might tell you at some point.' A phone vibrated in her pocket and she removed it. 'But that will have to wait.' She grinned at Claudia. 'Our other guests have arrived.'

My blood stuck in my throat. 'Who?'

My mother smiled at me. 'After sixteen years apart, it's time for our family reunion.'

26 CASSIE: AMY

There was no vegetation covering the back of the building, but it was easy to find the rear exit. Gabriel and I trudged through a damp alleyway, scattering cats from our path and stepping over soggy cardboard and squashed beer cans. Moonlight guided our way as I put fingers to my nose to fend off the stink of rotten food seeping through the concrete.

My father stopped me from opening the door.

'What you smell is the aroma of death and it comes from this building.'

'That's all the more reason to get inside and rescue Alice.' I shook his hand off me. 'Or do you want to abandon your daughter if she's in trouble?'

His eyes had sunk further into his skin. The darkness consuming his face had grown stronger since we'd arrived in the city.

'You don't know what's in there and we have no plan. This is madness, Cassie.'

'So, we leave Claudia inside? Is that what you're suggesting?'

He wiped the sweat from his forehead even though the night was cold.

'No, of course not, but I should go in first, and then call you when it's all clear.'

I tried not to laugh, but couldn't help myself. 'You can barely walk, old man. If anyone should wait here, it's you.'

As if to prove my point, he bent over and coughed as if he'd been smoking twenty a day all his life. I stared at him and hoped nobody inside could hear us. Claudia had said the exit would be unlocked. If it wasn't, I wasn't sure how we'd get in the building.

Gabriel righted himself and wiped the spit from his mouth. 'I've fought the hordes of Hell, killed demons in the hundreds, and defied the Creator. I think I'll be okay against whatever Mary has cooked up in here.' He held his hand out to me, but I didn't take it. 'It's you I'm concerned about, Cassie.'

'Fine. But I'm more worried about what's happening to Alice behind these walls. And I won't leave Claudia alone after she's risked her life for me.'

I turned from him and pulled the door open. There was no going back now. Claudia's text had said to head straight down to the lowest level, and someone would meet us there. She didn't say who, but I guessed she was getting help from at least one member of the Foundation; she had a way of making friends quickly.

It was dark inside, but noises came from the other end of the corridor. I dragged my father into the shadows as a group of four teenagers wandered from one room to another, all seemingly normal until the girl appeared, covered in bees apart from her head.

Gabriel's chest trembled and I could see he was about to cough again. I put my hand over his mouth as we pushed our backs into the wall. The shadows were long and I hoped they concealed us from the kids.

The other kids exited the corridor, but the bee girl stopped and turned in our direction. She held out a hand and bees drifted from her palm, heading right at us.

My fingers were still over my father's mouth as I watched the insects flying straight for me. I was about to pull Gabriel to the floor when a man's voice distracted the bee girl and she spun towards the room. The bees turned at the same time, re-joining her as she disappeared from our view.

I breathed a sigh of relief and removed my hand from Gabriel's lips. His chest was moving slowly as he clutched for air.

'That was close,' he said.

I considered leaving him there, but then thought better of it. There was a set of stairs to the right, so we took them and kept going until we reached the bottom. It was another long blank passageway, but this was a vacuum where you could hear a pin drop, so when Gabriel coughed behind me, I nearly jumped out of my skin. I turned to tell him off, the words caught in my throat by the sight of blood in his hands.

'What's wrong?' It was a stupid question, but I couldn't think of anything else to say.

He wiped the blood from his mouth and leant against the wall. 'I don't believe this English climate suits me.' His lips trembled as he smiled. 'I'd forgotten how cold it is in the north.'

'It makes the locals strong.' Her voice was low as she stepped from the shadows, a woman in her twenties wearing a white lab coat. 'I'm Amy. I work with Alice.' She handed Gabriel a tissue. 'And with your mother, Cassie.'

To my eternal shame, I forgot about Gabriel and put my hand on her arm.

'Are they okay?' My father coughed again and my guilt forced me to look at him as Amy answered the question.

'No, they're not, but in different ways.'

'What?' I was in no mood for riddles. 'And where's Claudia?'

'I'll show you; follow me.' She strode into the shadows. But I stood my ground and took my father's free hand.

'Perhaps you should stay here.'

'No, we have to see it through together.'

He was right; what choice did we have? We followed her to a lift and got inside. She pressed her finger against a panel and we descended. Amy leant against the back. I put my palm on the metal and the cold of the surface trickled through me.

I peered at her. 'You work for the Foundation?'

She nodded. 'I've been helping your sister for the last few weeks.'

'Helping her do what?'

'We've been cataloguing a database of supernaturals while Alice has analysed their blood and DNA.'

I stared at the Foundation logo stamped into the metal as the lift continued down. All I could think about was that warehouse where Bolt had waited for us. In my head was an image of the doctor cutting open Claudia's chest as others around him pursued medical procedures I tried not to look at.

'Why?' I knew Alice had always wanted to be a scientist and that leaving university and her studies had devastated her. Still, I couldn't understand why she'd be doing such work in this place after we'd stopped the nuclear apocalypse. Not after our separation. Why hadn't she tried to find me? Had she forgotten about me so quickly when she'd got her dream job here? Or maybe reuniting with our mother was all she'd ever cared about.

'Mary told Alice the Foundation wanted to prove a link between all supernatural creatures, as part of a connection to Darwin's theory of evolution.'

'What does that mean?' I said.

'That supernaturals and humans are related to each other biologically.'

'That's not what Mary wants,' Gabriel said.

Amy opened the lift. 'You're right.' She put a hand on Gabriel's trembling fingers and smiled at him. 'And you'll find the evidence in here.'

She led us into a giant laboratory full of scientific equipment. It smelt clean as if recently sterilised.

'Is my sister here?'

'We'll get to her soon, but you need to see this first.' Amy took us through another door and into a storage facility. It was as cold as a fridge, with an aroma of an autopsy.

'What is this place?'

She walked to the far wall and pressed her hand to it. An entrance slid open and we stared at its contents: six plastic vessels containing living things, all of which were at least seven feet tall. I stepped closer, my mind flashing back to the first time I was in the Nexus on Lindisfarne and the collection of supernatural creatures imprisoned there. On that occasion, all the specimens were unique, but these were the same: humanoid, but with long claws for hands and feet, hard scales for skin, fangs for teeth and, when I moved to see part of their backs, broad wings. They all appeared to be alive, but asleep.

'These are some of your mother's experiments.' Gabriel coughed blood over the floor as Amy spoke. She gave him another tissue and held his hand. 'Dr Silk started them from her notes when Mary disappeared, but she added the last components this week. Can you guess what living creatures she cannibalised to create these?'

I stared at them in their containers. 'She used harpies for the claws, mermaids for the scales, and some flying things for the wings, but what about the bodies?'

'They're human; what else?' Amy put her hand on a tube. 'But there was one final part Mary needed for them to be complete.' She banged on the glass and all four of them woke, staring at us with piercing purple eyes.

I gasped. 'She placed demons inside them?'

'Mary Arcane has lost none of her charms, has she, Gabriel?'

My father spat more blood on to the floor. 'Where is she?'

Amy nodded behind us. 'Through the door there.'

'Why has she done this?' All I could do was stare at this collection of Frankenstein monstrosities and wonder what my mother was doing with Alice.

'She claims she wants an army to defend herself against those who hunt her and, ultimately, use them to kill God. But I believe there's more to it than that. What do you think, Gabriel?'

Amy spoke to him as if they were old friends. But as I listened to her, a low humming noise crept into my ears. I scratched at them, but it didn't go away, only getting louder and crawling into my head. Was this what it was like to have tinnitus?

My father clasped at his throat and stumbled into a

container. It wobbled on its pedestal and threatened to drop, but stopped at the last second. But its occupant, and the others, were awake now, and every one of them glared at me through wide purple eyes. Amy and I grabbed Gabriel's arms and led him across the room to lean against a bench. He answered her question, but looked at me.

'Cassie, you must understand, she wasn't always like this. Your mother was a good person when I met her, but she suffered so much for so long something snapped in her. She's broken and nothing can fix her.'

I knew about being alone and abandoned, about being chased and hunted. 'I don't blame her for wanting to protect herself. Being pursued all your life would turn the gentlest of people into a paranoid wreck.'

'It's not just that, Cassie. Some things your mother has seen left her scarred for life.' He put a hand to his head. 'She told me about them and I still have nightmares. What she's gone through, none of us can understand.'

I didn't want to ask, but did. 'What did she tell you?'

He reached out to me. 'There was horror before the Flood for Mary. She was twelve when they first found her. She hid in the woods and watched an angel murder her father, one of the Heavenly Host killing another, all under the orders of God and directed by Michael. Her mother lasted four more years before Mary was orphaned, all alone until one of those tasked to kill her instead fell in love with her.' His tears were red, the life seeping from his flesh. I could feel it in his hand, see it in his eyes.

'Are you sure you want to see her again?' Amy said.

I held on to him as the hum in my head turned into thunder and it became difficult to focus.

My father smiled at me. 'I didn't before Cassie convinced me to come here.' He squeezed me and the din in my skull got weaker until it ebbed into nothing. 'Now I have to bring us all back together, to be the family we should have been.'

'Follow me, then,' Amy said.

And we did.

27 ALICE: BLACK BLADE

my came through the door, followed by Cassie. My
sister ran towards me, my name dying on her lips as
Silk struck her on the back of the head with a gun. She
stumbled forward. Her legs bent as she fell at my mother's
feet, near the babies in their jars. I strained against my
bonds, lifting the chair a few inches from the ground before
dropping again.

Next to me, Claudia's eyes burnt red as she snarled at
Mary.

'You and your human whelp will die for that,
Nephilim.'

My mother waved a hand at her. 'My, my, it's such a
long time since anyone used that as an insult against me.'
She removed something from her pocket and knelt at
Cassie's head. 'But I'm afraid you won't be doing much of
anything soon, little vampire.' She thrust the needle into the
back of Cassie's neck.

Claudia and I screamed together.

As I tried to contain the rage burning through me, a
sickly man staggered into the room, his chest stained with

blood and his face about to collapse in on itself. He stumbled towards my mother with his hand out. Then his legs crumbled and he joined Cassie on the floor.

'Who is that?' I said as Amy crouched in the shadows at the back of the room.

My mother stroked his head as he breathed heavily. 'Poor Gabriel; this wasn't how you expected it to end.'

'That's my father?'

She stood with the syringe full of Cassie's blood in her hand. 'What's left of him.'

Silk strode forward and pointed the gun at Claudia.

'The bullets in this will kill you, child, so stop straining.'

She stuck her tongue out at him. 'I'll chomp on your neck later.'

My mother waved the needle in the air. 'No more squabbling, children. There's important work to do.'

'What are you going to do with Cassie's blood, Mother?'

She went to the trolley with the Blade of Reality in the glass cage. She put the syringe down and removed the Blade.

'You hear this singing to you, Alice, don't you? I see it in your eyes.'

The hum was louder in my head, bouncing off every part of my skull so my brain felt as if it was inside a microwave, slowly going to the maximum heat.

'What have you done?'

She got her scalpel and detached the silver side of the Blade so I saw its organic insides. The sinew and bones vibrated, and my mind was about to explode.

'I've injected your blood into the Blade's biological system. That's why you can hear it calling to you. It will be interesting to see what happens when I add your sister's to it.'

My arms and legs were on fire. 'You used your children, weaponised us for God knows what.'

She laughed at me. 'Was that a pun, Daughter?'

'What are you babbling about, Mother?'

She brought the Blade nearer to me so I got a close-up sight of its organs pulsating and breathing inside the metal.

'When I showed you this, didn't you wonder where the organic material was from? Didn't you ask yourself who would create such a thing, and how?'

'I had more important things on my mind.' Like wondering how Cassie had turned into such a monster. How was I so blind I couldn't see they'd faked those video clips?

She ran her fingers through my hair. As well as my brain boiling, it was as if my guts were inside a washing machine.

'I forget how much of a child you still are.'

'Are you going to spill the beans about that little sword or what?' Claudia spat the words at her.

My mother pushed the vibrating Blade at Claudia. 'Or maybe I'll chop off your head with this?'

'Do your worst, Nephilim.'

'That word again.' She returned to me. 'Which brings us back to where this all started. Can you hear it calling to you, Alice?'

She was right. I could. At first, it was noise, but now, if I focused on it, I'd swear it was speaking to me. But I couldn't understand it and it felt as if my ears were bleeding.

'What is it saying?'

She shrugged. 'I don't know. We'll ask your father when he wakes up.'

I glanced at him. He was breathing slowly with his face buried into the floor. 'How would he know?'

'Because he's an archangel, silly, and all the Heavenly Host have a direct line to the Creator.'

'You mean…?'

I couldn't say the words. She held up the Blade so we could all see its organs moving.

'Yes, God made this with bits of Their body. I'm holding a part of God in my hands. No wonder the Blade could cut holes in reality and transport its holder anywhere. It's telepathy and teleportation working together, attuned to the mind of the bearer. Once I inject Cassie's blood to mix in with yours and God's, we'll be able to use it to find the Creator.'

It sounded like a terrible idea. 'And then what?'

My mother laughed. 'Why, we'll use the Blade to kill the Creator. Then I'll be free at last; we'll all be free.' She grinned at me. 'The Blade, which has a direct link to God, has a connection to you two now. You don't need to see where They are; you can go straight to Them. One of you will do this for me.' She ran a finger over the edge of the Blade, making sure she didn't touch the flesh of the Divine. 'What would you do, Alice, to protect Cassie from the petty wrath of the All-Powerful?'

I gritted my teeth. 'I'd do anything to save my sister.'

My mother held up her hand and I noticed the spot of blood on her skin. 'Indeed. So why are you so surprised with me doing this to protect myself?'

'Because it's monstrous and I'll be no part of it.'

'Oh, you will, daughter of mine. I promise you that.'

The straps bit into my skin, but didn't budge. 'I'll never do it.'

Her face bulged with anger. 'Imagine how you'd feel if the Lord God our Creator decided you were an abomination and was so determined to kill you, They murdered millions of others in the process. You wouldn't be so judge-mental then, Alice. I have no choice but to protect myself.'

'So Cassie and I are only an experiment for you, some-thing you can weaponise?'

She shrugged. 'All parents use their children in some way or other. I'm just doing it for survival.'

'You can't do this to our daughters, Mary.'

Gabriel crawled across the floor, talking to her but looking at me. Then he reached Cassie and held on to her head.

'It's too late for you to stop me, Gabriel. If you'd helped me years ago, like I begged you to, then I wouldn't have had to hurt anyone.' Mother bent forward and grabbed his shoulder, hauling him up with ease. 'But I found out what you were doing with that nurse, how you plotted against me.' She threw him across the room and into the wall. 'If I hadn't fallen into a coma, then none of this would have happened.' She lifted Cassie and laid her on to the trolley next to the Blade of Reality. 'Still, seventeen years later is better than never at all.'

I screamed as she plunged the syringe into the Blade's organs, injecting Cassie's blood into it as my head burnt. I tried to channel my anger and pain to spark the Arcane inside me, but it was fruitless. All I could do was shout at her.

'I won't use it for you, Mother.'

She nodded at Silk. He strode forward and pushed the gun into Cassie's temple as she lay on the trolley.

'One of you will do it, or I'll kill the other. It's that simple, Alice.' She stared straight at me. 'I'm not running anymore, no more hiding. I'm not waiting in fear for God's return. You should be glad to do it, Daughter. Otherwise, the Creator will undo all Their work. They won't rely on a

Great Flood this time because fire and brimstone will sweep the planet until every living thing burns. Their favourite angels in Heaven will survive, and then they'll start all over again. There'll be no free will, only an iron fist beating everything into God's submission. You can save the world from such a fate, Alice. If you don't, what comes after this will be on you.'

A fire was burning through me and I'd never felt so useless in my life. Where were my Arcane abilities? In a last desperate attempt to do something, I searched deep into my mind for them, slumping in the chair when I got nothing.

Then the heat cooled inside me as the air turned cold. My mother and Silk were peering at flesh and blood undulating inside the Blade, so they never noticed the group of bees crawling across the floor.

But I did.

The bees on the ground multiplied in number until they swirled in the room and flew towards Silk and Mary. The doctor threw up his arms to protect his face, but she just stood there and grinned as the flying hum covered her head like a yellow and black blanket.

A loud bang heralded the door being thrown open, and Astomi ran into the room. The others followed him as he grabbed hold of Silk and hurled him into the wall. Melissa held up a hand and the bees returned to her. Then Yuki-Onna lunged at my mother, spraying ice and snow all over her until she looked like a frozen statue.

Dr Silk picked himself up and shook his head. 'You kids shouldn't have got involved. What happens now is your fault.'

He reached for the gun on the ground, but he wasn't quick enough to stop Sandy from grabbing his face.

'Sleep now, Doctor.'

Silk's eyes glazed over, and then he slumped to the floor.

The four of them, my friends, stood there and smiled at me. Silk was out cold and my mother was just cold. Was she dead? If she was, how would I feel?

I pushed the thought from my mind and looked at Cassie. As I did so, the block of ice that was my mother exploded, throwing icicles all over the room, hitting my friends and knocking them over.

A few particles cut into my face. The pain made me flinch, turning my head to my mother as she dusted herself down. There were a few bee stings on her cheeks, but otherwise little evidence she was injured.

She glanced at Silk on the ground. 'Julius will be pissed off.' She peered at my friends as they helped each other up. 'Now you'll see what my project is made of.'

'Stop this, Mother, before it's too late.'

She laughed at me. 'It's already too late, Alice. Look at Julius and see the fruits of your work come to life.'

I dragged my gaze from her to him as he stood. First, Silk removed his uniform, and then his shirt. Then, as all eyes were on him, he flexed his shoulders and held out his arms. His slim body transformed into one a bodybuilder would have been proud of, with muscles popping out of him like Popeye. But even that wasn't the strangest thing about him: from his back grew a perfect pair of sprite wings. As I sat there with my mouth wide open, the wings beat so fast, he was able to lift off the ground.

'What did you do, Mother?'

She grinned at me. 'It's what you've done, Alice, not me.' My mother left the Blade on the table and came to me, putting her fingers on my cheek. 'You're such a clever girl, my daughter.' She glanced at Gabriel. 'I wonder which of us you inherited that from.'

I jerked my head from her touch. 'You took my findings and injected supernatural cells into Silk?'

My mother nodded. 'It was Julius's idea. He'd conducted a lot of experiments with human-supernatural hybrids while I suffered in Hell, most of which were unsuccessful, but he was keen to volunteer for this.' She watched him floating above my friends. 'We started with two blood types, the sprite and the troll, but I see they've exceeded all of our expectations.' She returned her focus to me. 'What do you think, Alice?'

Before I could reply, Yuki-Onna sent ice flying from her fingers straight into Silk's face. While she did that, hundreds of bees stung his chest and arms. His body hung in the air and trembled, his feet shaking as they dangled just above the ground.

Then they stopped and everything in the room fell silent; all apart from the constant drone coming from the Blade of Reality.

28 ALICE: ULTIMATUM

The hum vibrated inside my head before being overtaken by the sound of Silk howling beneath the ice and the insects. Then he flew at Melissa and Yuki-Onna, grabbing each of them by the throat and lifting them off the ground.

Sandy and Astomi threw themselves at him, pulling on his legs to drag him down. But it was no use. He kicked them away with ease. They hit the back wall with a loud crash, slumping there and unmoving. Then he hurled the girls into the same spot, so all four of my friends lay there in a heap.

My mother clapped her hands. 'Make sure they don't move, Julius, while I finish what I've started.'

She touched my face again before returning to the thing containing God's flesh. Then she injected Cassie's blood into the Blade, and Cassie screamed with me.

The fire had returned to my veins as my sister twisted and jerked on the floor. My father held his hand out to her, but he couldn't move. My mother had the Blade above her head as the hum increased inside my brain until it was about to explode.

'Stop this!' I shouted.

But she didn't, lowering the Blade as she moved towards me. 'Only you can stop this, Alice.' She smiled at me. 'Dracula told me you never break a promise. Is that true?'

I wanted to smash my skull against the wall.

My vision was blurred as I looked at her.

'I always keep my word. So what is it you want?'

'You know what it is, Alice. Promise me you'll take this Blade and kill God. If you do that, I'll spare your sister and all your little friends.' She glanced at Claudia. 'Even that annoying vampire.'

'And if I don't?'

My mother shrugged. 'Then I'll have to do it myself. But only after I've watched Julius kill everyone in here.' She twisted her neck to peer into the shadows at the back of the room. 'Yes, even you, Amy.'

I focused on her words, trying to shut out the noise in my head, but it was impossible.

If I threw myself at Claudia and drank her blood, would I have enough time to use my Arcane abilities to defeat my mother? I glanced at Silk gazing at me and knew I'd never get the chance.

My mother held on to the Blade and I understood I had no choice but to do what she'd asked. I was about to make that promise when the noise in my head lessened and I heard something else there.

Reach out to your sister. Call for Cassie and she will help you.

I glanced at my father. Was that him speaking to me?

Did it matter?

No.

I didn't say the words in my mind. I didn't say anything at all. All I did was recall all the memories I had of Cassie, from our first meeting in the park until our last time together when Lucy separated us.

Dozens of images turned into hundreds in an instant, and each of them was of my identical twin sister and me. They poured through my brain until they were the only things I thought of.

Then Cassie moved.

Her body jerked up from the trolley, her fiery gaze burning red as she leapt at Silk. She grabbed the doctor by the throat and tossed him across the room. He crashed through a table, sending test tubes and instruments all over the floor. He rolled to the side, springing up as his arms and legs expanded until he was larger than the trolls I'd fought.

Silk lunged at Cassie, but his new bulk must have thrown him off balance as she dodged him easily. He bounced off a chair and growled.

Had Cassie's Arcane abilities returned somehow? She'd been the stronger of the two of us during Lucy's training, but that was because the Devil was secretly feeding their blood to my sister.

The memory of it made me cringe as Silk beat his wings and lifted until he was above her. His body was enormous, like some great beast dragged up from the depths of the ocean.

Cassie inched back from him as he floated towards her. His gigantic hands were heading for her throat when he stopped in mid-air. The hum had died down in my head and there was a new noise now. It was like the sound a jet makes as it flies overhead on a cloudless day.

I looked at my sister while Silk glanced at my mother.

Then he exploded into a hundred pieces, with bits of him hitting every corner of the room. Cassie was quick enough to protect herself, but one of his arms landed in my lap while his blood covered my legs. I jerked up to dislodge his limb from me, glancing at Claudia, who had a colossal smile on her face as well as a lot of Silk's blood.

'Well, I guess it wasn't a successful experiment after all,' my mother said.

She carried the Blade from us and went to what she'd created: her Alisium. Their eyes blazed yellow like stars in the night sky, a violent illumination which peered at me. Then Cassie crumbled to the floor, and Claudia and I yelled in unison.

Despair rushed through me as I watched my mother put the Blade of Reality back together, the silver shining and vibrating to the same beat throbbing in my skull. Her face glowed with mania, thousands of years of fear and frustration coming to the boil inside her. My head dropped; I was ready to give up when I felt the hands behind me and the knife cutting me free. When I was loose, I turned to see Amy cutting Claudia's bonds.

'We have to get out of here,' Amy said.

I went to her. 'No, we have to stop my mother.'

'She can't use that weapon without you and Cassie, so, as much as I'd love to snap her neck right now, it's probably prudent to get the two of you away from her. Plus, your sister's injured,' Claudia said.

Both of us ran to Cassie while Amy helped Gabriel up.

I put my hand under her head.

'Cassie, can you hear me? It's Alice.' I stroked her hair and ran a finger over her damaged ear.

Her eyes blinked awake. 'Some birthday party this is.'

Claudia and I got her up as Amy carried my father towards us.

'How are you doing that, Amy?'

She didn't answer, but put Gabriel down and he threw his arms around his daughters. We weren't like that for long because the floor vibrated and the whole room shook.

I ran to my friends as they woke from what Silk had done to them.

'What happened?' Melissa said as I helped her up.

'I'll tell you later, but we have to get you out of here first.' Then, the ceiling and the walls cracked around us. 'This place will collapse soon.'

They all nodded, helping each other as I returned to my father. Tears filled his face as he gazed at Cassie and me.

'Mary has poisoned the Blade. It will implode and take this building down with it. You have to leave now.'

In the corner, my mother was swinging the Blade through the air and everything it touched melted. Tables and chairs buckled under its gaze, dripping onto the floor as she grinned. Two white-uniformed members of staff stumbled into the room and she passed the Blade over their heads. The flesh ran from their bones into a puddle at my mother's feet. I watched them melt away, unable to hear their screams over the noise in my head and the walls crumbling around us.

I couldn't leave her with all that power in her hands.

'No, I have to stop her. There's no telling what she'll do with the Blade, even without us.' My mother held it at her side as she went to the Alisium, running her free hand over the jars and smiling at them. Would she use them to kill God?

'That's our mother?' Cassie gripped my fingers.

'We have to leave,' Amy said. 'We need to evacuate the

building. There are young children and families here, plus all the staff.' As she spoke, screams erupted above.

'Go,' Gabriel said. 'I'll stop her.'

She must have heard him. 'No one is leaving.' She moved near us, the Blade shimmering in front of her. How could we stop that? We backed off towards the far wall, but she kept on coming. 'You and I will kill God now, Alice, or I'll slaughter everything in this room.'

What choice did I have? At least I could use the Blade to get her and it away from this building before it came down on all of us. All I had to do was use it to cut a hole to anywhere but here.

But that wouldn't help everyone else in the Foundation.

The screaming from above continued amongst the cacophony of the collapsing walls. Then, as I thought about surrendering to her will, a blur sped across my vision and grabbed one jar of the Alisium.

Then it stopped moving: it was Claudia.

'Hey, last of the Nephilim, do you love these freaks more than your real children?'

My mother spun, the Blade cutting through the air and sending a shock wave through my brain. Cassie and I shrieked together. Before my mother could attack Claudia, Gabriel was on her, forcing her to the ground.

'Go!' he shouted at us.

Amy grabbed my hand and Claudia was at Cassie's side in a flash. Amy dragged me towards the exit, stumbling behind my friends as they rushed through the doorway. I turned to see my parents grappling on the floor, rolling over like long-lost lovers as the Blade of Reality transformed into a vast golden glow. I'd seen something similar before when Lucy and Michael had converted to their pure archangel forms in battle. It was burning my eyes as Amy pulled me out and up the stairs.

'We have to make sure everyone is out of this place.'

We followed her up, Claudia helping Cassie, who still hadn't recovered fully. Amy and I checked what rooms we could as the building shook around us. Fittings fell from the ceiling and walls, pipes burst and water ran everywhere. All the time, my head continued to scream.

Finally, I stumbled outside to find Claudia and Cassie on the pavement with groups of Foundation staff and residents huddled behind them as sirens wailed in our direction. Melissa, Sandy, Yuki-Onna, and Astomi were leaning against a wall, catching their breath.

Cassie grabbed me. 'We have to go back in for them.'

She was correct: we did. But I also didn't want to. And I didn't know why.

Wasn't this what I'd searched for: to be reunited with my parents; to find my mother? I'd found her and we'd bonded, but all along, she'd used me.

And she wanted me to kill God.

It seemed there was a lot of that going around.

I stared at my sister, wondering how I could have ever doubted her.

I nodded. 'Yes, let's save them.' I took her hand, ready to run back inside when the building collapsed.

We fell to the floor as bricks and mortar crashed in front of us. Glass shattered as debris flew into the air, leaving a cloud of dust everywhere.

Claudia rushed to us. 'Are you okay?'

Cassie and I lay there, holding hands and facing each other. The concrete turned to rubble across the road, and a swarm of dirt and debris swirled through the night sky. My sister and I stared at the destruction as I wondered if either of our parents had survived the mayhem.

'Can you hear it in your head, Alice?'

'No, it's gone now.'

'It's the same for me.'

We stayed there and hugged, the lie burning into me. The sirens were nearly on us when we separated.

Cassie smiled at me. 'We have to go before the police get here. We're wanted fugitives, remember.'

'You don't have to worry about that anymore,' Amy said.

I peered at her. 'Who are you?'

She took her name badge and dropped it to the ground. Then her face shivered and bent, transforming into someone else.

'Not Amy. I'm Natasha.' She held out her hand to me. 'I was a nurse at the Foundation before you were born.'

I took her hand. 'It was you who removed us from the hospital, who saved us from Lucy and Michael?'

She shook my hand and did the same with Cassie. 'Gabriel asked me to do that once he discovered what Mary was up to. I was supposed to keep you together, but I knew it would be too dangerous that way. So I had to separate you.' She stared at us both. 'I'm sorry.'

I threw my arms around her. 'Thank you, Natasha.' I let go. 'But what do you mean we don't have to worry about being wanted fugitives?'

'I hacked into the police database and wiped all their records of you two. Most of them shouldn't be looking for you now, at least not countrywide. I tried it with the government group AEGIS, but their security was too strong.'

'So, you're a shapeshifter?' Claudia said.

'And you're a vampire,' Natasha replied.

I left them talking and pulled Cassie away from the

smouldering ruins of the Foundation. The emergency services turned up with their spinning lights looking like a kaleidoscope bursting in front of us.

'What do we do now?' my sister said.

I didn't know.

But something whispered to me from the dark corners of my mind.

THANK YOU!

Thank you, dear reader for purchasing this book.

If you enjoyed reading about Alice and Cassie Arcane their journey continues in these books:

The Arcane Supernatural Thriller Series
Book one: The Arcane
Book two: The Arcane Identity
Book three: The Arcane Quest
Book four: The Arcane Ultimatum

Many thanks to my wonderful wife for all her support and patience.

My eternal gratitude to Wendy Cross for being the first person to read the Arcane and who gave me essential feedback on the characters and the plot.

Extra special thanks to Karina Gallagher for being a dedicated reader of my work.

236   THANK YOU!

The Arcane Ultimatum edited by Alison Jack.

Cover design by James, GoOnWrite.com

ABOUT THE AUTHOR

Andrew French lives amongst faded seaside glamour on the North East coast of England. He likes gin and cats but not together, new music and old movies, curry and ice cream. Slow bike rides and long walks to the pub are his usual exercise, as well as flicking through the pages of good books and the memoirs of bad people.

Find out more at www.andrewsfrench.com

Facebook:

https://www.facebook.com/A-S-French-Author-150145625006018

Twitter:

www.twitter.com/andrewfrench100

Instagram:

www.instagram.com/andrewfrench100

And replies to all his email at mail@andrewsfrench.com

If you have the time, please leave a review at Amazon or Goodreads

Thank you!